The Language of the Son

Laura Moe

Laura Moe Books   Seattle, WA

The Language of the Son

Contact information: www.lauramoebooks.com
Twitter@Lauramoewriter

Instagram @Lauramoewriter

Book clubs: for discussion questions visit www.lauramoebooks.com

Cover design by Ashley Nicole Conway @ANconway

Summary-.

Subjects: *Still reeling from his breakup with Shelly, Michael focuses all his attention on navigating his father's world, but the future may not hold everything he's hoped for. All his life, Michael has longed to know his biological father, but now that he's living in his house, proximity might not be enough to bring them together.*

Contemporary YA—Fiction | Love—Fiction | Relationships—Fiction | Climate change—Fiction | Coming of age—Fiction | Parents—Fiction | Families—Fiction | Friendships—Fiction | Young Adult—Fiction | Seattle—Fiction | Writers—Fiction | New Adult—Fiction | Environment—Fiction

DDC- FIC

ISBN 9781077682429

It is a wise father that knows his own child.

William Shakespeare

The Language of the Son

By Michael Gillam Flynn

I don't know how to speak the language of the son.
There's a vernacular for my father carrying me on his
shoulders for a better view,
A slang for choosing the right mitt. I don't know them.
He never taught me the jargon for hooking a fish,
Or the patois of the ancestral story.
I have yet to translate the dialect that accompanies a cer-
tain look
And the mother tongue between men.

I have not learned the words Dad, Daddy, Pa, Pop,
Papa, Baba, and father.
The verbs to mend, to rend, to shave, to drive, to love, to
protect
feel foreign on my tongue.
How do you speak the language of manhood
with the man you have never met?

Chapter One

My father crouches nose to nose with Jack, his seven-year-old Golden Lab, as they mock wrestle in the back yard. I'm kind of jealous because he's never played with me like that, but I have no right to be; he's known the dog longer.

Two weeks ago, when I moved in with my father, I imagined conversations where we discussed books and movies and compared memories of Rooster, Ohio. So far none of the films inside my head have followed the script.

His wife Jennifer stands next to me at the French doors. "Your father morphs into a big kid when it comes to that dog." Lucy, Jennifer's black and white Boston terrier, trots over. She picks up the dog and nose kisses her. "I'd be willing to bet if he had to choose between me and Jack, the dog would probably win."

She sets Lucy down. "I'm headed out to get a haircut. Do you want to come? There's a Barnes & Noble near the salon."

I glance at my father and imagine more of our awkward dialogue—or more precisely—our silences. Conversations with him are like throwing darts in the dark. "Yeah, I'll go with you."

Laura Moe

Jennifer steps outside and Lucy shimmies next to her to the back yard. "Ash, I'm going out, and taking Michael with me."

My father looks up, blows her a kiss, and yanks at a rubber rhinoceros inside his dog's jaw. He doesn't even glance at me.

Jennifer hands me her keys. "I'll let you drive if you like."

I give her a big smile. "Awesome. I like taking the bus, but I also miss driving. In Rooster, if you want to go anywhere you *have* to drive."

"There aren't any buses there?"

"They only run in the center of town, and not very often."

"Do people bike?" she asks.

"Not if they want to live long."

She laughs, and we head out to the garage.

Her shiny, red Toyota Camry isn't even the same species as The Blue Whale.

As Jennifer gets her hair cut, I browse the magazine section of the bookstore and do a double take at the cover of *People* magazine. Ryan Gosling has the same highbrow, shadowy stubble, and chiclet teeth as my father. *I* look like my father. So why the hell don't women fawn over *me* like they do Gosling? Or my father? Oh yeah, because I'm kind of a nerd.

I place Ryan Gosling back on the shelf and peruse the writing magazines. The current issue of *Writer's Digest* exclaims I should, "Write That Novel Now!" The three-week writing workshop I just finished taught me enough to know I am nowhere *near* ready to write a novel.

I meander through the bookstore shelves.

In the poetry section *100 Love Sonnets* by Pablo Neruda reminds me of Shelly. Don't want to think about her. That ship has sailed and hit an iceberg.

Over in nonfiction several of my father's books occupy half a shelf. His latest book deems him the 'Dr. Oz of the ocean world.' He's everywhere. On paper anyway.

After an hour of browsing, I choose a writing guide called *Ron Carlson Writes a Story* and a gift to send to my sister Annie: *100 Great Novels to Read Before You Die.*

Jennifer walks in as I'm in line to pay. "Do you mind if I look around a little?" she asks.

"Not at all." I'm never in a hurry to leave a bookstore, even a half-assed one like Barnes and Noble. "I'll wait in the cafe."

As a school librarian, you'd think Jennifer would be sick of books, but their bookcases at home are full. And she'll read pretty much anything. The other day I caught her reading *Fifty Shades of Grey* in the backyard.

"This book is hysterical," she said, when I handed her a bottle of water from the fridge. "It's so bad I can't put it down."

"Are you learning anything?"

She closed the book and unscrewed the cap on her water. "Don't worry. I won't tie your father up and whip him." She winks. "At least when you're in the house."

While Jennifer shops, I pour myself a free cup of water and find a seat. The book I bought for Annie lists a couple of my favorites, *The Grapes of Wrath* and *Heart of Darkness,* but I don't see *Shadow of the Wind. On the Road* made the cut. Shelly's favorite book. The one that binds her to Theo.

Theo. That two-timing-lying-asshole and my latest nemesis.

Why is it the people I care about most betray me? Rick. Shelly. Theo. I wonder who's next.

As much as she hurt me, not being with Shelly every day is like phantom pain, as if I'm missing a leg yet I still want to run.

After I met my father for the first time, and he and Jennifer asked me to stay, I thought remaining in Seattle was the answer to everything. I wouldn't have to encounter Shelly and I'd get to know my father.

Now I'm not so sure.

First, I don't know what to call the guy. He's my biological father, but he's not my dad. Jennifer calls him Ash or Ashton, but those names feel too familiar. And I'm sure as hell not going to call him Love Monkey or any other pet names Jennifer uses.

If I were one of his students, I'd call him Dr. Meadows or Professor, but since I'm not, I don't address him at all.

Jennifer sets her bag on the chair across from mine. "I'm going to get coffee. Do you want something?"

I start to stand but she gestures for me to stay. "I'll get it. What would you like?"

"Unsweetened iced tea."

I'm well into the first few pages of my book when Jennifer returns with my large iced tea. Technically she's my stepmother, but that label doesn't quite fit. She's more like a cool teacher I've been hanging with.

"Nice haircut, by the way," I say. It looks the same as before, but I remember how Shelly always expected me to notice *her* hair.

Jennifer swivels her head and touches her nape. "Thanks."

She's one of those women who rocks short hair. Maybe it's her long neck and large brown eyes. She's tall and lean and really good-looking for an older chick.

I gulp down half my tea. "What did you buy? *Fifty-One Shades of Grey?*"

"Ha!" She picks up her bag and slaps the book on the table. "*Kafka on the Shore.* It's for book club."

I skim the book and hand it back to her. "Murakami. We read *Norwegian Wood* in my Contemporary Lit class last spring."

"If it's any good I'll loan it to you when I'm finished." She slides the book back in the sack and coils her fingers around her cup. "It's nice having a live-in bibliophile," she says. "Ash rarely reads fiction, so I can't talk to him about the novels I read."

From what I've observed, my father's primary interests are his wife, the dogs and cat, and the ocean, and maybe not in that order. "If my father were a book he'd be written in a foreign language."

Jennifer reaches across the table and pats one of my hands. "Give him time. This is new to him, too."

She removes the white cap on her cup and blows across the top. She clicks the lid back in place and takes a sip. "Your being here reminds him of a confusing time in his life."

"High school *is* one of the nine circles of Hell."

Her lips curl into a half smile, and she nods. "It isn't high school per se that haunts him. His father's suicide splintered their family, emotionally and financially."

I stir at the ice in my drink with the straw. "The day I met him, he told me he hadn't been back to Rooster until I contacted him."

"None of his family has."

"Maybe I should return to Rooster for now and come back at a better time."

Jennifer sips again and blots her mouth with a small white napkin. "There's no such thing as a better time. You just have to live each day with what life throws at you."

I tilt my head and study her. "I can see why he likes you, and it's not just because you're hot."

She strikes a pose. "I am pretty fabulous. Maybe someday you'll get lucky and meet someone like me."

I raise an eyebrow and grin. "One can dream."

She swirls her drink and takes a long gulp. "In a way you and Ash are both suffering from a sort of culture shock. You're living in a strange house in a strange city, and Ash hasn't been a father before now. At least not to a human being."

"Maybe I should crawl around on all fours, shake my ass, and bark so he can relate to me better."

"You'd just end up being Lucy's bitch."

I throw my head back and laugh. "Why is it so easy between us?"

"I've worked with teenagers so long I'm one of you."

"It's more than that," I say. "I feel I can talk to you."

"I'm the impartial observer. You and Ash have huge stakes." She gestures between the two of us. "The stakes for us are pretty low."

I guzzle the rest of my drink and consider this. "You're a librarian. Are there any books or manuals on how to talk to a stranger who happens to be my father?"

"There may be, but the best thing to do is let the relationship evolve on its own terms."

***

As we walk to the car, I say, "I haven't been able to write since the program ended."

She reaches into her bag and digs for her keys. "You're probably on sensory overload. There's even a name for it: PTSE. It stands for Post Traumatic Somatic Experiencing. Your senses were overstimulated and your brain is trying to realign itself. But unlike PTSD, it's easily fixed."

"Will I be normal again? Not that I was ever *normal,* but normal *Michael* could at least think in complete sentences."

"Eventually." She hands me her car keys. "Remember, you're also experiencing the trauma of meeting your father and his fabulous wife."

I chuckle and flip the unlock button.

"Don't force your way out," she says. "Take it one day at a time."

"Yeah, but I still have this portfolio project to do in order to get college credit for the workshop. We have to connect writing to another discipline, so I need my writing muscles to flex again."

Jennifer buckles herself into the passenger seat. "Talk to Ash. He can give you some science ideas."

I start the car. "Or maybe I can arrange an audience with the Pope."

She rolls her eyes. "You two need to find some common ground. I can't be the go-between forever."

"I'm trying."

"I know you are."

We run a couple of errands and arrive back at the house late in the afternoon. My father isn't there. Jennifer picks up the note he left on the kitchen counter and reads it. "Looks like he's off doing chest-beating activities with his cronies."

"I'm going to try to write," I announce.

"Don't get mad at yourself if you can't."

I wave it off and walk up the two flights. My bedroom is a converted attic with hardwood floors, a double bed, desk, and a dresser. I even have my own bathroom with a shower. It's nicer than the room I occupied back at Earl and Dot's, yet the Sutton's house felt more like home.

My father's three-story house overlooks Green Lake. Funny how, while I was attending the summer writing workshop, I often passed this house when I ran around the lake. I had no idea I was so close to him.

I set the books I bought on the small bookshelf in my room. Since moving here, I haven't accumulated much other than the beer fridge my workshop roommate left for me. Don't want to grow too comfortable in case things turn to shit. Besides, I have no idea how long I'm staying.

I fire up my laptop, but nothing comes from my brain, so I open my email.

There are several messages in my inbox, including ones from Earl's wife Dot, my sister Annie, and my brother Jeff. Nothing from Shelly. Not that I expect one.

I open Dot's message first. She and our custodian Earl took my sister and me in after Earl discovered I was living in my car. They're officially Annie's foster parents.

Hi Hon,

Earl and I hope you're enjoying your stay in Seattle and getting to know your father. We all miss you around here, even though Earl would never admit it. He's been extra busy these last few days since school is getting ready to start in a few weeks. He's been barking orders at the new custodian to get him trained. When you come home you should apply to be a substitute custodian. Earl would really enjoy giving you orders again.

We added two more hens recently because, I'm sad to say, Myrna and Joy were killed by a coyote. We keep the girls penned up all day now unless one of us is home.

I'm teaching Annie how to can. Last week we set up some corn and green beans. We had a bountiful harvest of both this year.

If you decide to stay there permanently Earl and I would understand, but we want you to know you're always welcome here.

Much Love,

Dot

PS. Annie misses you terribly, especially since she and Kyle broke up. She has other news, too, so you should give her a call ASAP.

I feel bad for my sister. And poor Myrna and Joy. Of all the chickens, Myrna was my favorite. She was the boss.

I punch up Annie's number on Facetime. "Heard about you and Kyle."

"Unlucky in love must run in the family," she replies.

"Looks that way."

She pauses, then asks, "Did you read Jeff's and my emails?"

"Not yet. Why?"

"There's more bad news."

My heart pounds and I pop a couple of antacids in my mouth. "Did something happen to Mom? Or Shelly?"

"No, but you might want to sit down for this."

"I am sitting."

Annie takes a deep breath. "The Blue Whale got stolen last night."

"*What?*" I bolt up from my desk chair. "Who the hell would steal a nineteen-eighty-two Ford LTD station wagon?"

"Maybe some guy who needed a place to live?" Annie says.

"Very funny. How did it happen?"

"Jeff borrowed it when he and Kayley moved into their apartment. He said he got your permission to use it."

"He did."

"Well, after he unloaded it, he parked it on the street, and yesterday morning the car was gone. Jeff feels really bad about it."

I scrape my free hand through my hair. "Oh man, I loved that car. But it's not his fault. The locks on The Whale didn't work."

"I'm sorry, Michael."

"Yeah. Me too. News from home just gets worse and worse."

She fills the screen with her face. "That's why you should never, *ever* come back here."

"Apparently."

She draws her phone back. "How are things going with your father?"

I pause. Annie barely remembers her own father, who died when she was three. Of the three of us kids, Jeff's the only one who knows his dad. "Kind of weird."

"Weird in what way?'

"It's… hot and cold. It's not *bad*. It's just… odd."

"It really does suck to be you right now, doesn't it?"

I chuff a laugh. "As usual."

We talk for a few more minutes. After I sign off, I text my brother.

-I heard about The Whale. I'm not blaming you. The locks were broken.

He texts back. *Dad will have another car for you when you come back.*

I open my photo app and swipe through pictures of The Whale. Most of them include Shelly standing nearby. All I have left of both of them now are photos.

***

Around six, the aroma of cooking wafts upstairs and I head down to the kitchen. "That smells great, Jennif…." I make an abrupt stop.

My father wears a cook's apron, sautéing vegetables in a cast iron skillet. Jennifer is nowhere in sight.

He picks up a glass of white wine on the counter and takes a drink. "Jenny tells me you don't eat chicken, so I'm using beef."

"Oh, thanks." I consider telling him about Myrna, but don't want to sound stupid.

Jennifer comes in the door carrying a handful of fresh herbs from the garden. "Did you get any writing done?" She sets the parsley and sage near the stove.

"No." I perch on a stool and slump my shoulders. "But I found out my car got stolen."

"Oh no! Not the Blue Whale!"

My father gives us both a bewildered expression as he shreds the herbs with his hands and tosses them in the pan.

"She was an enormous old blue station wagon," I tell him. "My sister named her The Blue Whale."

"I see." My father nods and sets down his wooden spoon. He wipes his hands on the apron. "*Balaenoptera musculus* is the largest and noisiest mammal in existence. It can grow to a hundred feet long and weigh as much as one hundred and seventy tons. Its low-pitched moans can be heard for miles." He swigs his wine.

I give him a sad grin. "Sounds about like my car."

"They're endangered, but not facing extinction," he adds. "Because of its size an adult blue is rarely attacked."

"Unfortunately, *my* whale was. She probably got stripped for parts."

Jennifer lifts the open bottle of white wine and tops off my father's glass. She fills another wineglass and hands it to me. "Sounds like you need this."

"Thanks."

Jennifer rests her chin on my father's shoulder and inhales. "Smells delicious, babe."

He grins and snaps off the burner. "Almost ready."

She glances at me. "Michael, will you help me set up so we can dine outside?"

"Sure."

She and I carry plates, silverware, napkins, a bowl of fruit, and the wine and spread them out under the umbrella table. The dogs follow us to the yard and Jennifer tosses each of them a gnawing bone. "That'll keep them from begging for about a minute and a half."

My father brings out a medium-sized bowl of rice and a large plate containing stir-fried beef and vegetables and places them on the table. "Let's eat."

Jennifer kisses him on the cheek. "Thank you for cooking tonight, hon."

We all sit down, heap our plates with grub, and begin to eat. "Earl would say we're eating like cave people."

My father snickers and nods. "Sounds like Earl." I often forget my father also knew the custodian from when he was in school.

The three of us eat silently for a couple of forkfuls. Then my father says, "Sorry about your car."

I feel a tremor of grief. "I considered The Whale a friend. She rarely gave me trouble."

My father loads his fork. "My favorite car was the cherry red Mustang I drove senior year in high school. Until it got totaled."

"What happened?" I wonder if my mother ever got to ride in that car. In her diary she said my father once gave her a ride to work after school.

He swallows his bite. "It was in spring, a few weeks before graduation, and a bunch of us got drunk at a party. I got too toasted to walk, let alone drive, so I let one of my less inebriated friends drive. But he rolled it into a ditch."

"Wow. Was anyone hurt?"

"No. That's the extraordinary part. There were eight of us inside the car. Since we were packed in so tightly, nobody moved when we landed upside down." He stirs the food on his plate. "The guy driving got a slight concussion, but the rest of us walked away unscathed."

I look at this man, whose face is an older version of my own, a man who plans his words before he speaks, and it's hard to picture him as a drunken teenager.

"How about you?" I ask Jennifer. "What kind of debauchery did you experience in high school?"

Jennifer primly sets her hands on her lap. "*I* was a perfect angel in high school. Just as I am now."

My father snorts. He points to her as I take a swig from my wine glass. "*This* one got herself kicked out of the school library for two weeks."

I just about spit out my wine. "The future librarian got booted out of the library?"

She takes a lady-like sip from her glass and gives us a Mona Lisa smile. "There were six of us together during study hall, and we noticed that a guy at the next table fell asleep. One of his shoes was untied, and my friends dared me to creep over and tie his laces together. So, I did. When the bell rang and the kid tried to walk, he fell right over."

"How did he know it was you?" I ask.

"My so-called friends ratted me out. But we all got bounced out for two weeks."

My father tastes his wine and sets his glass on the table. "Tell Michael about the pencils."

Jennifer's eyes brighten. "I was the *master* at sharpening pencils to razor thin points. And when teachers weren't looking, I'd shoot them up at the ceiling tiles where they'd hang like darts."

I laugh. "Did you ever get caught?"

She shakes her head. "I was one of the smart kids, so teachers never suspected me. I got away with all sorts of stuff like skipping class and wandering the halls."

I cross my arms and sit back in my chair. "You were kind of bad ass."

My father looks at his wife with admiration. "She still is. Under all those layers of cuteness resides a little devil."

She strokes his cheek with the back of her hand. "And you love that about me."

He kisses her fingers. "Indeed, I do."

Clearly, I'm the third wheel, but it doesn't bother me much because, so far, this is the best conversation my father and I have shared.

He looks over at me. "When you choose your wife, find one who is not only smart and beautiful, but also a little scary. She'll keep you guessing every day."

It figures my first bit of fatherly advice is for me to find someone like Shelly.

Chapter Two

I consider telling Shelly the latest news about The Whale. That car was more than just transportation; it was a big part of our relationship. She's the first person outside the family who learned I was in living in it, and she didn't judge me.

I lean forward, click Compose, and begin to type.

Dear Shelly
So.
Life, huh?

Annie told me she ran into you at Walmart, and when she mentioned I'm staying with my father you burst into tears and squeezed the breath out of her. So, I guess you're happy for me, and maybe you still love me a little.

I want to say moving in with my father is the happy ending to my story.

His wife says to give it time. I get along great with her, so living here is okay. Jennifer says summers are his busiest time, and he's doing a lot of appearances to promote his new book. He was on Good Morning America and CBS This Morning last week.

I'm tempted to have Annie send me my mother's journal so I can reconnect with the guy he used to be. But he's probably not that guy anymore.

Just like I'm not the same guy you met last summer, and you're not the same girl.

Who the hell ARE we now? How can we become such different people in such a short period of time? Maybe betrayal changes a person. And now that the workshop is over, I have too much time to think about us.

That day at the light rail, before the shit hit the fan, you said you hoped we could find a way to reinvent us. Us 2.0.

In a way distance and time have done that for us.

You remember my friend Shoe? The one who texted you after I blocked your number? Of all of the friends I made at workshop I miss him the most. He almost talked me into forgiving you for sleeping with Theo.

Almost.

My hand hovers over the keyboard. Should I sign off with *Love, Michael*? Do we still love each other?

I highlight the entire message and delete it. I don't know what to say to her.

Chapter Three

The morning is perfect for a run: a light drizzle falls like liquid velvet on my skin. I take a whizz, brush my teeth, and change into running gear. As I descend the steps, I overhear Jennifer. "You need to spend time with him. Get to know him."

I stop on the stairs and wait for my father's response, but he mumbles something I can't make out. I continue down and traipse into the kitchen.

"I'm going for a run," I announce.

Jennifer nudges him. "Maybe Michael can join you today, Ash."

He raises his travel mug and glances at me. "I'm already packed and ready to hit the road. Maybe next time?"

I shrug. "Sure."

He kisses Jennifer and slips out to the garage.

My father's refusal to connect with me loops through my head, and I imagine him saying, 'I didn't ask to be this kid's father.'

Yeah, he doesn't want me here.

But I'm not ready to go back to Rooster. What's left for me there? A shattered love, a broken family, and a stolen car? In a couple of years Annie will leave. My brother Jeff's on his own now. And none of us can save our mother.

You'd think breaking her arm by tripping on debris would send a message to shovel out her damn house.

Last I heard from Jeff's dad, Paul, everything is the same. But at least Paul got Mom to see a counselor.

Shelly used to tell me my job was to be the kid, not the parent. I could use some of her half-assed advice about my father right now.

In spite of the weirdness with my father, life here in Seattle gives me a sense of hope. I don't feel like a freak. All my life I've been the weirdest kid in the room. I grew up as white trash but was too well spoken not to be a bully target. I made a couple of friends with my AP classmates, but I never took anyone home. Not even Rick. He'd been like a second brother through middle and high school, yet he never saw the inside of my mother's house.

I will find a way to stay in this city, with or without my father.

The blood fueling my brain feeds me images of finding a job, moving into my own place, writing in a coffee shop. Maybe Shoe and I can share a place when he comes back.

I pull out my phone and call him.

"Hey, Flynn." Shoe says. "Why do you sound like you're in an iron lung?"

"I'm running. What are you doing?"

"Sitting on the porch, melting in the heat."

"How hot is it?"

"Ninety-five degrees with 95% humidity," he says.

"Ouch! Have you been writing?"

"Not a word. It's like my brain got sucked out on the flight home."

I slow my pace. "Yeah, every time I try to write a thick fog rolls in."

"Same here. I carry a dictionary with me in case I need a more complex word than 'the.'"

I laugh. "Not that I'm glad you can't write either, but I feel less alone."

"I hope my brain reboots soon."

"My father's wife says there's a name for our condition: Post Traumatic Somatic Experiencing."

"Is there a cure?"

"Time. And not forcing ourselves to write."

"Hopefully I can write again by the time school starts this fall," he says.

A pair of girls paddle by in a canoe. They wave, and I wave back. "And you're definitely coming back here?"

"Yep. I really like Seattle, and the UW campus. And I loved screenwriting."

"I thought poetry was your passion."

"It is, but a guy's gotta eat. At least with screenwriting I might actually get paid."

"Are your parents okay with you moving back here?"

"Not at all, but my being away all summer gave them a taste of the empty nest. They survived it. Are you going to hang around Seattle?"

"Maybe."

"How are things going with your dad and stepmother?"

I hesitate. "I haven't known them long enough to assign parental labels."

"What do you call them?"

"I call *her* Jennifer."

"What about your dad?"

"I don't call him anything. Calling him Dad, Father, Ash or Ashton feels false. I guess I could call him Dr. Meadows." I side-step a large branch in the path.

"Maybe devise a nickname for him. Like Science Guy, or Turtle Dude. Hey Turtle Dude, can you pass the salt?" I laugh.

"Or you could just call him Doc."

"That's not a terrible idea."

"Ask his wife what you should call him."

"Thanks, I will." After a couple of yards, I slow my pace to a jog. "So, in your email you said you and Shelly still text one another."

"I'm not trying to hone in on your girl. I'm gay, remember?"

"I know."

"Aren't you in contact with her?" he asks.

"Not since that day."

"Sorry, dude," he says.

"Yeah, well, it's like you said, I attract critical story lines. My life is a telenovela."

"I should take notes and write a Netflix series based on your treacherous misadventures," he says.

"Someone should profit from it."

After Shoe and I sign off, I sprint the last mile. By the time I make it to the house, my body swims in sweat. Jack's Cat follows me upstairs and curls himself on the bathroom rug as I shower. I like that he's adopted me as a member of the family. Jennifer told me one afternoon Jack discovered the cat in some bushes near Green

Lake, its face mangled from indefinable abuse. She and my father took the cat to the vet, where they removed part of one eye, but the cat seems to manage well without it.

The aroma of coffee wafts up as I trot down the steps. Jennifer sits in the kitchen reading *The Seattle Times* on her iPad when I shuffle in. I pour myself a glass of water from the Brita pitcher and sit at the breakfast bar.

We greet one another, and I pour myself a bowl of Uncle Sam cereal with coconut milk. The cereal is probably meant for constipated old geezers. Each serving has 10 grams of fiber, but I like the taste. Meals in my father's house are far healthier than what I ate in Ohio, yet I still miss Dot's butter-laden home cooking.

Jennifer sets a mug of coffee down and I perch across from her. "How's life treating you today?"

My mouth is full, so I wave my hand to and fro.

"Your father is in Pacific Beach, so you're stuck with only me for a few days."

"Book tour stuff?"

"This time it's work." Jennifer fills a coffee cup for me and slides it across the counter. "If you'd like you can help me at school today."

"You work in the summer, too?"

"*All* teachers work in the summer. I stop in every other week or so to check my mail, process new books, update the operating systems, and work on lesson plans."

"Librarians have lesson plans?"

She gives me a spiky look. "We don't just check books in and out. We're responsible for teaching you evil teenagers how not to just Google everything. Not every-thing on the internet is *fact*."

"Sorry. I didn't mean to imply…" I raise my hands in defeat. "I'm not sure what I meant."

"You meant to imply librarians are superfluous and we only sit around reading magazines."

"No. I love the library. I guess I never thought about what you actually *do* all day."

"If you come to school with me today, I'll show you."

I hold my hands out as if being handcuffed. "Now that I pissed you off, I guess I kind of have to."

She grins and pretends to lock handcuffs around my wrists. "You bet your ass."

"Sorry."

She gives me a dismissive wave. "It's okay. Most peo-ple don't appreciate our role in education." She eyes me. "Besides, you have nothing better to do."

I scratch my head and glug some coffee. "True.

She glances at the wall clock. "How soon can you be ready?"

I empty my mug and plunk it on the countertop. "Ready."

"Hard work will take your mind off your troubles."

"Spending a summer day working inside a school." I tap my chin as if contemplating. "What a novel idea."

We both grin at the veiled reference to my community service last summer. Which I spent with Shelly. Damn. Why does everything make me think of her?

Jennifer lets me drive again and the GPS guides me to her school. We walk into the building and Jennifer heads toward the office. "I need to check in at the office." Jennifer greets an iron-haired woman sitting behind the front desk. "Hi Greta, how's your summer going?" "Good," the woman says. "Mandy came up with the grandkids last week." Greta gives me an inquisitive eye. "Greta, this is my stepson, Michael, from Ohio." "Mercy. I didn't know your husband had kids." "Life's full of surprises." Jennifer winks at me and saunters over to the mailboxes. Jennifer's mail is in a crate. "Michael, I need your muscles to carry this to the library for me."

"There are also some boxes in the library for you," the secretary says.

Jennifer claps her hands together and jumps up and down like a kid. "Ooooh. Her-cu-leees! Her-cu-leees! New books!"

Greta and I chuckle. "You really *are* an overgrown kid," I say.

The Library Media Center is at the far end of the hall-way, and by the time we make it there, the crate weighs five hundred pounds. I dump the mail down with a thud on the circulation desk and Jennifer immediately rifles through it. "I love snail mail. Even junk mail. It's like get-ting gifts every day."

We sort through the envelopes and magazines. "Let's make three piles: magazines, keep, and recycle," she says.

"My mom would keep all of it. She'd claim it was useful in some way."

Her eyes travel over me. "I'm so sorry, Michael. How old were you when she started hoarding?"

"Nine or so. About a year after my sister's father was killed."

Jennifer nods. "I've heard hoarding often begins after a traumatic event. As if people try to hold on to something they can't quite define." She slaps a stack of *Sports Illustrated* on the magazine pile. "You've suffered many blows for someone so young."

"My fiction teacher at the workshop was envious. He said the best writers suffer a lot." Talking about Theo bugs me, yet in spite of Theo being a despicable human being, he *is* a good writing teacher.

Jennifer quickly assesses each piece of mail, and when the 'recycle' pile grows taller than the 'keep' pile, I haul it out to the recycling bin.

When I return, Jennifer holds a box cutter above the taped seam on top of one of the boxes and slices across it. She opens the flaps and lowers her face inside. "There's nothing like new book smell, is there?"

I poke my head in and inhale the scent of paper and glue. "It smells like nirvana."

"Old book smell is nice, too. It's heavy and musky, as if reeking of knowledge."

"If they bottled it, I'd wear it as cologne," I say.

"Then you'd be a chick magnet for geeky girls like me."

I study her for a second, looking elegant even in a T-shirt and shorts. "I would never call you a geek."

"You should have seen me in high school. I was a beanpole with braces. The only boys who paid attention to me were John Steinbeck, William Faulkner, and Richard Brautigan."

"You didn't date in high school?"

"I hung around with a few geeky guys who also loved books. But I wouldn't call any of them boyfriends." She pulls a handful of books out of the box. "I didn't have my first kiss until I was a freshman in college."

"Wow."

She gazes longingly at the large screen on the back wall, as if scenes with him are projected there. "His name was Tony Aqui and he was a boy in my Freshman English class. He was my first kiss, my first everything. He used to quote Shakespeare sonnets to me."

"Girls dig poetry." Shelly and I shared Pablo Neruda's poetry and books. The ache of losing her grows shallower each day, yet I can't imagine it won't leave a scar. "What happened to him?"

She shrugs and sighs. "We outgrew each other."

Jennifer pulls a wheeled cart out of her office, and I help her check the books off the invoice. It takes us about twenty-five minutes to unload three boxes because we both keep stopping to page through the books.

"If we worked at Amazon," she says, "we'd be so fired."

"Yeah, I'd be reading entire books before I packed them."

"If you see any you want to borrow, just pull them off the cart. I won't catalog all of them today."

She opens a file on her desktop computer and shows me what looks like encrypted messages from space. "These are catalog records. In the old days they were typed on small cards and stored in card catalogs."

I glance at the screen. "Do you do this for all the books?"

"For every item in the library. It tracks what we have, the number of copies, the material type, the age of materials, and their locations. We can also see how often something circulates."

"I guess that's why it's called library science."

She forms a gun with her hand and points it at me. "Bingo."

Jennifer tasks me with placing a barcode on the back, stamping new books with *Evergreen High School* inside the cover, and on page thirty-five. "Also write the barcode number on page thirty-five."

"Why page thirty-five?"

"It's a random number, but if the barcode on the back of the book gets damaged, we can still find the record from the inside cover or that page."

As I finish books, I place them on a cart for her to enter into the database. Each of us accumulates a small stack to borrow.

I pick up a CD set she selected. "I've never listened to a book on CD before."

"It keeps me from getting road rage in Seattle traffic."

I read the back of the CD out loud. "*Jesus' Son* is a collection of ten stories narrated by a young man recovering from alcohol and heroin addiction." I look up. "This doesn't sound like a kid's book."

"I keep adult materials on hand for teachers. And some of my kids are mature readers, so I'll put pretty much anything on the shelves."

"Even *Fifty Shades of Grey*?"

"Well, not *everything*. *That* one is getting donated to Value Village." She glances up at the wall clock. "It's 11:30. Let's wrap this up and have lunch."

She locks the remaining books and the cart in her office.

After we eat, we stop at home and take the dogs for a walk around Green Lake. If I were walking alone, I'd break into a run.

Jennifer must sense my restlessness, because she says, "you don't have to stay at my pace. When Ash and I walk he usually runs ahead and we catch up at Peet's coffee."

"Okay. I'll see you there." Once I increase my pace my muscles gratefully comply, as if they've been stopped in traffic, and the lanes finally started moving.

Running fires up the neurons in my brain. For some reason I recall a line from the Jane Hirschfeld poem I read in my poetry workshop. *I want to gather your darkness in my hands, to cup it like water and drink.* The words make me think of Shelly and how we blended our darkness to create light, the black heat of our souls igniting a fire. Never before had I felt such intensity, but now the flames flicker and sputter like a candle at the end of its wick.

Will I always feel like I'm shot full of holes?

The coffee shop comes into view and I double back and meet Jennifer and the dogs. I slow to a walk and file in next to them. "Want me to take the reins?" I nod toward the two leashes.

"Sure. Thanks."

After a few steps, I ask, "How long did you and Tony Shakespeare date?"

Jennifer gives me a curious glance. "Most of my Freshman year."

"Was it something specific that broke you up?"

"Why are you asking me this?"

I look down at my feet. "I'm in the aftermath of a bad breakup, and I guess I want to know how long it takes to feel human again."

She nods. "Let's go have a cup of coffee and talk."

We walk the last few yards in comfortable silence and cross the street to *Peet's*. The dogs lap from outdoor water bowls before we go in and order.

Jennifer gets a large iced tea for me and a cup of coffee for herself. Back outside, we find a table in the shade. I lift the lid of my drink and guzzle a quarter of my tea.

"So, you want to know about Tony and me." She removes the lid and blows on her coffee before taking a sip. "Somehow between graduating from high school and entering college I kind of blossomed from being a gawky giraffe into a young woman. And boys noticed me. Since I had *no* experience, I avoided the handsome cocky ones. I wasn't ready for guys like your father.

"Tony was nerdy and impossibly sweet. We were friends for a long time before we even held hands, and by the time we got physical, I totally trusted him. He was comforting to be with, like a pair of jeans that fits every time you slip them on."

"Sounds perfect. Why did you break up?"

She looks downcast. "I broke his heart."

"I'm almost afraid to ask how."

"If you were one of my students, I wouldn't be telling you this, but I think of us as friends as well as family." Jennifer replaces the lid on her cup and rests her manicured hands on the metal table. "Like me, Tony was also a virgin, and with him, everything was new. The first taste of a boy's lips on mine, the first skin to skin contact. Each moment with him was like discovering a new country, or a new flavor. We couldn't keep our hands off each other.

"And his quoting poetry just elevated the senses. He was an English major, and we talked endlessly about books and poetry. We often had to shove books off the bed before we slept together." She gives me a sly grin. "He and I mashed a few pages."

Heat creeps up my face. Images of Shelly and me on our final day together in the shower pop into my head.

Jack rests his head in my lap and snaps me back to the present.

"Being with Tony unleashed the power of my body, and it gave me the confidence to flirt with the handsome boys. Since I had never drunk alcohol before college, I didn't know my own limits. One evening that spring, when the longer days and warm air fueled my hormones, we

31

went to a party. I drank too much of the wine punch and started dancing with some graduate student. I didn't even know his name, but he said all the right things. I was wearing a skimpy sundress and his fingers knew the right places to touch me."

I stroke Jack's head. "Are you sure I should hear this?"

"Don't worry, I didn't sleep with him," she says. "But I did kiss him, a long soulful kiss that may have ended up being more if Tony hadn't come outside. He'd been in the house chatting with a friend of ours, and he brought me a plate of food. He was always so thoughtful that way, and there I was scaling this tall, handsome guy like an animal, with no way of hiding it."

"Did you break up that night?"

"No. He pretended to forgive me. I think he tried to, anyway. But he never looked at me quite the same way again. And I always felt the need to apologize whenever I was with him. Anyway, over summer he transferred to Arizona State and I never saw him again. Back then, before Facebook and Instagram, it was easy to lose track of people."

I pitch my elbows onto the table. "Do you ever wonder if you and he could have made it?"

She looks down and swirls her cup. "Sometimes. But ultimately, we were both wounded by what I'd done, and some wounds are impossible to heal."

I stir the straw around in my iced tea, wondering if I can ever get over Shelly's betrayals.

The Language of the Son

Jennifer takes the lid off her cup again and takes a long drink. "I know all of your friends have gone home, but you should go out tonight. See a movie or something."

"You'd be okay if I abandoned you?"

"One of the reasons Ash and I work so well together is we allow each other a lot of space. When one of us needs to be alone or work something out, we'll either work long hours, or take off for a few days."

"Is that what he's doing now? Working out what to do about me?"

She secures the lid back on her drink. "That may be part of it. He wants you to stay, but he needs to reconfigure his role as a father."

"I don't expect money or ...."

Jack nudges Jennifer's hand. She reaches down and ruffles through the dog's fur and kisses his nose. "Or what? What *did* you expect once you met him?"

"I have no idea. All my life I felt this emptiness inside me from not knowing who or where he was. And now that I'm here, I don't have a plan."

"Neither does Ash."

"Well, we have *that* in common."

Lucy pushes Jennifer's hands away from the other dog. "You two are more alike than you know." Jennifer pets her dog and gives her a nose kiss, too. "What did you know about Ash before you met?"

"From Mom's diary, I learned about this awful girlfriend he had in high school."

33

"Ellie." She squinches her face. "Ash told me about her and showed me pictures. Even when she smiled, she had resting bitch face."

"Did he say why he stuck with her two years?"

"Her father was *his* father's business partner, and Ash's and her parents were best friends. He said it just made life easier to keep dating her."

Jack places his head between my knees and I stroke him. "My mother wrote in her journal that he felt pressured to major in business so he could take over one of his dad's companies. But that's not what he wanted."

Jennifer nods. "His father's suicide was sort of a dark blessing for Ash. He was free to be himself."

"He told my mom he wanted to be a beach bum."

"Ha! In a way he is. He just gets paid well for it." She eyes me. "What else did you know?"

My fingers graze through Jack's fur as he flaps his tail against my thigh. "He was in track. And he smoked pot. And he and my mom secretly met for sex in the prop room under the stage."

Jennifer lays her palms on the table. "Ash feels bad about how he treated your mother, but you know how stratified society is in high school, especially in small towns."

I chew on some ice. "I guess resent him for that. My mom has a long history with men who abandon her one way or another." I snap the lid back on my tea and drink through the straw.

Jennifer crosses her legs. "He didn't know about you. If he had, things would have worked out differently. I don't know if your father would have married your mother, but I'm certain Ash would have been present in your life."

I let this sit for a while. My father had nothing to do with Bob's death, or how my mother reacted to it. The seeds for her choices are buried deep in her roots, before she knew Ashton Meadows, or any of the other men she loved. "How do I let myself not be angry?"

"Ash will hate this idea," she says, "but family therapy might help."

I make a face. "He's not the only one."

She shakes her head. "Two peas in a dysfunctional pod."

Chapter Four

We return to the house and the dogs settle down for naps in the living room. Jennifer sets out to run an errand and I step out to the back yard with the book I bought yesterday.

After the intensity of the writing workshop, the pace around this house is almost too calm. Which may be a good thing. Since I've been here, I haven't once gotten wasted and thrown up in the bushes.

But I miss the friends I made on campus.

I sprawl in a lawn chair, prop my feet on the opposite seat, and take a nap. I wake to a crash from the kitchen.

"Motherfucker!" I hear a male voice yell from the kitchen.

My father stands at the island looking perturbed. A large pot dripping with sauce sits to his right, his white T-Shirt splattered in red splotches as if he's been shot. The front of the stove drips with sauce, noodles drape from the oven door handle, and small, snakelike piles of spaghetti lie on the floor. The normally spotless kitchen looks like a war zone.

"I thought you went out of town," I say.

He looks at me with a glassy expression. "Came back early."

I don't want to annoy him any further, so I don't say anything else.

My father closes his eyes, takes a breath, and says, "Looks like I should have stayed in Pacific Beach."

"Want some help cleaning this up?"

He wipes his hands on his spattered shirt. "That would be great."

"Where do we start?"

He scans the mess and sighs. "First, let's dump the noodles and what's left of the sauce in the compost bin."

I help him scoop most of the sauce and spaghetti into the large pot and carry it to the backyard compost container. My father fills a bucket with warm, soapy water. We dig around under the sink and find some rags to wipe the stove.

"Feels like I'm doing community service again," I say. "We spent a lot of time wiping down the classrooms."

My father dumps his rag in the bucket and gives me a long look. He wrings the water out, and asks, "What was most valuable about that experience?"

I want to say meeting Shelly, but after all the recent crap, the jury is still out. Yet if it weren't for her, I wouldn't be picking up spaghetti in my father's kitchen. I dip my rag in the water and twist out the excess. "I guess I learned that all messes can be cleaned up eventually."

He nods. We continue to wipe and rinse and I wonder if that's true. Things between Rick and me have never been the same since I tried to blow up his car. Shelly and I can't go back and erase her betrayal, or my reaction to it. And I won't ever speak to Theo again.

I also can't imagine my mother being able to remove the literal mess in her house.

"What was it like working with Earl?" he asks.

"He's a ball buster."

My father chuckles. "I'll bet he's a kitten underneath all that bluster."

"He is. His wife softens him."

"Wives have a way of doing that."

He and I continue cleaning the stove in silence and drop stray pieces of spaghetti noodles in the sink.

Jennifer steps in from the garage carrying a bag from Whole Foods. She scans what's left of the mess. "Did you guys have a food fight?"

"Yeah, and the spaghetti won," my father says.

She shakes her head and sets the groceries on the counter. "Some guys will do anything to get out of cooking dinner."

"I'd offer to cook," I say, "but the only thing I know how to make is peanut butter and jelly."

Jennifer pulls a bottle of Cabernet Sauvignon out of the wine rack. "Should we open this bad boy?"

"Hell, yes." My father sends the remaining noodles down the disposal and chucks his rag in the other sink. He grabs the stems of three wine glasses and opens the bottle with their electric wine-opener. He pours one for each of us.

Jennifer lifts her glass. "What should we drink to?"

My father grins. "To getting out of cooking?"

She taps a finger to her lips. "How about to discovering your son?"

A tense look crosses my father's face, yet he raises his glass. "To Michael."

The three of us clink our wineglasses, but the moment feels hollow.

My father sets his wine down and swabs the stovetop. Jennifer stows the groceries away while I mop the floor. When the kitchen is scoured, my father drapes his rag on the sink. "Well, I don't think I totaled the kitchen. How about I change clothes and treat us all to dinner. How does Italian sound?"

Jennifer nips some spaghetti sauce from his hair and licks her finger. "You might want to take a shower first, babe."

He kisses her, swats her butt, and says, "back in a flash."

I look down at my wet clothes. "I should probably change, too."

Jennifer rides shotgun, and I sit on a dog blanket in the back seat as my father drives his 1999 Subaru Outback Legacy wagon. An affinity for old station wagons must be genetic. I feel a pang for The Blue Whale. My father drives like I do, too: left arm resting on the open window, steering with his fingertips.

Jennifer cocks her head. "Are you going to tell me how spaghetti ended up all over the kitchen?"

"I was at the stove, pouring freshly rinsed noodles into the marinara just as Jack and Lucy lunged between my legs and forced me off balance, where my elbow shoved the pot off the stove. I tried to catch the handles, but as you saw, I didn't quite make it in time." He shows her his right hand. "And I burned a couple of fingers."

"Awww, poor baby." She lifts his hand and kisses his fingers. "All better now?"

He smiles at her and runs his hand over the back of her neck. "Totally, *mi chica*."

Why didn't I bring my ear buds or something to read? I redirect my attention to new construction along 85th Street.

"There is nothing as heavenly as the smell of Italian food," my father says, as we pull into the parking lot. "It's the smell of love and cheese and the reason to live."

A hostess seats us at a booth. My father and Jennifer share one side, and I face them.

"Everything here tastes great," Jennifer says.

My father skims the menu. "Why don't we share a pizza? I'm not sure I'm in the mood for pasta after my great kitchen disaster."

"Ooh, that barbecue chicken pizza we had last time was wonderful."

The waitress, whose name tag says Carrie, approaches. "Hey, Dr. Meadows. How's your summer going?"

He looks up. "Carrie. Good to see you." He beams at her, but not in the creepy way older guys sometimes do when scoping out pretty girls.

"I start my Master's program in the fall," Carrie replies. "Thanks again for the letter of recommendation."

"Excellent." He gestures to Jennifer. "Carrie, this is my wife, Jennifer."

The two women shake hands. My father glances at me and hesitates; a puzzled look crosses his face. "And this is..."

A beat later I shoot my hand out. "I'm Michael Flynn. From Ohio."

"I hope you're enjoying your visit here. Seattle's a great city." Carrie holds up her order pad. "Can I get you guys something to drink?"

My father closes his menu. "We already know what we want. A large barbecue chicken pizza and a pitcher of water." The waitress grabs our menus and disappears to retrieve our drinks.

Jennifer leans in, and whispers. "Ash, why didn't you introduce Michael as your son?"

"It's okay," I say. "I know the whole situation is odd."

Jennifer lifts a breadstick from the basket and points it at both my father and me. "You two need to figure your relationship out." She double taps her husband on the shoulder with her breadstick.

He picks up his own breadstick and the two of them sword fight. I grin and almost forget the awkwardness from a minute ago.

Carrie returns with a pitcher of water and three glasses. The waitress lingers when she places my father's glass in front of him. She touches his arm. "I just wanted to tell you your classes were the highlight of my undergrad program."

"Thank you, Carrie." He rewards her with his Hollywood smile. "That means a lot."

After she walks away, Jennifer rolls her eyes and pivots closer to me. "Before he met me, your dad was the Casanova of the Biology department. He still has a parade of pretty students throwing themselves at him."

His face flushes, and he pours himself a glass of water. "I do not."

She reaches over and strokes his stubbly chin with the back of her hand. "But how can they resist this hunk of a man? He's handsome, smart, and famous. A dangerous combination."

My father looks simultaneously pleased and embarrassed. He casts his eyes over Jennifer. "And what about you and *your* fan club?" He looks at me. "My wife neglects to mention her cadre of lovesick teenage boy and lesbian library volunteers."

"Smart *is* the new sexy," she says.

We spend the rest of dinner engaged in banter, and the pizza is amazing, but an uncomfortable sensation lingers inside me, as if I'm watching a film about someone else's life.

Back at the house I pull an Olympia beer out of my mini fridge, take a swig, and lie on the bed.

I rest the beer can on my palm and stare up at the ceiling. The cat leaps onto my bed and purrs. I scratch him behind the ears. He raises his head and tail to demonstrate his approval. The orange and white tabby, named Jack's Cat, stares at me with his one good eye.

"This is all Shelly's fault," I say. "*She* pushed me toward finding him."

The cat doesn't respond.

Instead, he settles onto my chest, and I set the beer can on the night stand. I stroke the cat's head with both hands as he studies me with his single eye. "All my life I looked for this person called father. Now I'm living inside his house, yet I'm still looking for him."

Chapter Five

In the morning, I walk the dogs over to Peet's to buy a bag of coffee since Jennifer forgot to get some at the grocery store. Jack pulls me along behind him and Lucy skitters alongside. The disappointment I feel towards my father lingers.

The dogs lap from the water bowl outside Peet's while I go inside to purchase the whole bean dark roast. On our way back, Lucy stops to poop, and I pull a small plastic bag from the leash pocket and scoop up the dog shit. I knot the bag and toss it into a nearby receptacle. This city makes it convenient to own a dog.

I yank Jack away from a poodle who does not reciprocate his interest and we trot back to the house. "Coffee to the rescue!" I announce, as I hang up the leashes.

Jennifer presses her hands together as if praying, and mutters, "Thank you." She opens the bag and scoops beans into the grinder and brews a fresh pot.

I slather peanut butter on toast as the aroma of dark roast fills the kitchen.

Jennifer sets out two mugs. "Let's sit out front this morning. I'm in the mood to watch the lake."

She and I carry chairs from the back and place them on the front lawn. There's a lot more activity in the front of the house thank the back from traffic, walkers, and the lake. Jennifer and I are camouflaged by shrubbery.

I retrieve the two mugs and my toast and bring them out front. I settle in and set my cup on the arm rest of the

Adirondack chair. "Before I came out here, my sister An-nie and I talked about how we both felt Rooster didn't fit us." I glance toward the lake. "I could live here."

"You already do."

"For now. You guys can throw me out anytime you like. You aren't stuck with me."

She laughs. "You just moved in. Let's wait and see how it all goes."

"*If* he wants me to stay."

She sips from her mug. "He wants you to stay. He just doesn't know how to express it." She cups her hands around the mug. "*I* want you to stay."

I lean back in the chair. "How did he act when I first sent my message?"

Jennifer tilts her head to one side. "We'd just come home from walking the dogs around the lake. Ash went to his study to check his email, and I was bagging up books to donate to the library. Suddenly, I heard this strangled sound coming from his office. I thought he was having a heart attack, so I dropped the books and ran to him. Ash was staring at the computer as if there was a ghost on the screen. He pointed to your email and asked me to read it."

She takes a drink from her cup. "I did, and asked him if this was true. Famous people get wacky claims all the time. Ash hesitated at first, and then said it was possible. I told him to contact you, but he wanted to check it out first." She sets her mug on the ground. "Ash was heading out of town for several book signings, so he left it to me to make plane and hotel reservations in Ohio."

"And you guys spent a few days in Rooster."

She nods. "Which was hard on your father. He didn't have great memories of growing up there."

I smirk. "One more thing we have in common."

She reaches out and squeezes my hand. A motorcycle rumbles by.

I furrow my brow. "But he was a rich, popular jock. How could he have bad memories?"

She gives me a sad grin. "Even the most popular kids hide behind a facade. Ash and his siblings had to pretend their lives were golden because their father was a well-known fixture in town."

Shelly once told me she play-acted at being part of the popular crowd to hide things that scared her about herself, so I guess this is true.

Jennifer gets up and takes our mugs inside to top them off. She passes me my cup and sits. "The truth is, your father's life improved after his father's death."

I swallow the last bite of toast and set my plate on the grass. "But didn't they lose everything?"

She nods. "Yet the family stopped walking on eggshells."

Living with secrets does weigh on you. A ten-thousand-pound burden lifted from my soul when I finally revealed to Shelly that my mother was a hoarder, and later, when Earl learned I was living in my car.

She swats a bug away from her face. "Ash isn't a nervous flyer, but he was jumpy on our way to Ohio. It had been nearly twenty years since anyone in his family had been back in Rooster. They scattered like ants after his father's suicide, and they didn't look back."

"Did he tell you anything about his relationship with my mother?"

She sips her coffee and purses her lips. "Prior to your note, he never mentioned her. He told me about Ellie and his college girlfriends."

"I guess my mother wasn't worth mentioning."

She sets her cup on the arm of the chair. "Quite the contrary. When Ash spoke about your mother, he told me they had an underground relationship, and he treasured their time together. She was the one person he could be real with."

"Yet he never acknowledged her."

Jennifer is about to respond but her phone rings, and she dips inside to talk to whoever is on the other end.

After I finish my coffee, I go back inside and set my cup and plate by the sink. Jennifer is just finishing her phone call. She sets her phone face down and I fumble with a gold ring sitting on the counter. I slide it on my ring finger. "Whose is this?"

Jennifer sighs. "Ash is always leaving his wedding band lying around."

Like an idiot, I ask, "Why? He wouldn't cheat on you, would he?" Her face drains of color, and I immediately regret my stupidity. "I didn't mean…"

"He takes it off when he goes running and forgets to put it back on." She taps on the side of her cup. "I suppose if the conditions were right…there are some things beyond our control."

"I didn't mean to imply anything." Yet he *did* cheat on his high school girlfriend with my mother. I slip the ring off and place it in her palm. "I don't think he'd cheat on you. If he did, he'd be the biggest idiot in the universe."

She spins the ring on her thumb. "I believe his true mistress is the sea."

"He's crazy about you."

"I know." She places the ring back on the counter. "But your father *is* like a long mystery novel."

I hunch my shoulders. "Shelly used to tell me I was a book with missing pages."

Jennifer rests her elbows on the counter and cups her face with her hands. "Is she the recent breakup?"

I nod.

"Tell me about her."

"It's a long story."

Jennifer picks up her coffee mug. "I'm in no hurry."

I shrug and reveal the whole mess with Shelly and Theo. How when we flew out together, Shelly arranged for us to stay with her ex-boyfriend a couple of days before I moved into the dorm. And how she spent two *more* days at his place before meeting her parents in Hawaii. Then on her way back to Ohio, she asked me to meet her at SeaTac, where she revealed she not only cheated on me with Theo, but some random guy in Maui. My reaction to all of it doesn't make me look good, either. I screamed at her (check You Tube for 'airport Starbucks break up') and punched Theo in the face.

"I'm so sorry, Michael," Jennifer says. "Have you talked to her since?"

I shake my head.

"Don't take this the wrong way, but why did you agree to stay with Theo?"

I chuff a laugh. "Because I'm a moron." I rake my fingers through my hair. "I should have known what would happen. The day we landed, I spotted this guy in Baggage Claim who looked like a Hemsworth brother, and Shelly leapt into his arms."

"That had to hurt."

I shake my head. "This is all my fault."

She opens the dishwasher. "You had no way of knowing what would happen."

"I guess she and I weren't meant to last." I pour myself a glass of filtered water. "The first day Shelly met me, she discovered I was living in my car. I didn't even know her last name, yet she kept my secret and bought me breakfast. Then we were inseparable. And if I'd never met her, I doubt I'd be standing here in your kitchen."

Jennifer loads my empty plate and cup in the dishwasher and closes the door. "Funny how one seemingly small event sparks a major one."

I gulp my water and refill my glass. "Did my father say he was in love with my mother?"

She turns and props herself against the sink. "He's been pretty reticent about his feelings for her. He may not even know."

"Doesn't that bother you?"

"That he may carry a torch for a girl he knew in another lifetime?" She crosses her arms and wears a melancholy smile. "No. Each of us is filled with a past. Your father isn't the first man I loved." She pushes off from the sink and reaches for two apples. "And Shelly won't be the last girl you'll love, either."

"It feels like it, though."

She places an apple in my hand. "Everything takes time."

"How long did it take you to get over Tony Shakespeare?"

She bites into her fruit and thinks for a moment. "About six months. I'll always have a soft spot for him, but I learned to move on."

I crunch on my apple. It's the perfect combination of firm and sweet. "I like talking to you. You always make me feel better."

"I like your company, too. If I had a son, I hope he would have turned out like you."

Between bites, I ask, "do you plan to have kids?"

She gives me a pinched smile. "Ash is concerned there are already too many people on this fragile planet. We agreed not to burden the world by adding more."

"You'd be a good mom."

"Thanks, but I think I get my fill of the mom role with all my kids at school." Jennifer opens the fridge and grabs a water bottle. "Do you want to hang with me again today?"

"Sure." I chomp the rest of my apple and place the core in the compost bin under the sink.

Jennifer lets me chauffeur her to various errands. We buy dog food at Mud Bay and then go to Sky Nursery. As I carry two hanging baskets to the car, Jennifer says, "there's a great dog beach near here. Let's take the hounds there."

She tells me to follow the signs to the Kingston Ferry. "But stay in the left lane, otherwise we'll end up in line for the ferry."

"That might be cool."

"Have you taken a ferry yet?"

"On my first day in Seattle, Shelly and I went to Bainbridge Island." I drive past a marina with a yacht club and massive boats. "We're not on the poor side of town, are we?"

"Nope. But the beach is free."

We park in a paved lot that separates two beaches, and I ask Jennifer why the beaches are split.

"The beach on the right is for people. The one on the left is for dogs."

"It's nice the dogs get their own beach."

She clips a leash on each dog and walks them to the entrance. "Seattle is very pet friendly. We like our animals more than we like each other." Once inside the first gate, Jennifer unhooks the dogs' leashes and Jack spins in circles. She grabs his snout, and says, "You're such a happy puppy, aren't you? Yes, you are." Jack swats his tail impatiently against my leg as Jennifer lifts the handle to open the second gate. She barely opens it when the dog springs away from us. "He *loves* the beach."

Lucy remains nearby as Jennifer re-latches the gate. We walk down the sand toward the water. Lucy breaks away when a black lab invites her to join a small pack of dogs. All along the beach the animals tussle with one another, and a few, like Jack, dive right into the water.

"He swims pretty well," I say.

"Ash often takes him along on his trips. Your father's favorite place is underwater."

"Maybe he was a sea turtle in his last life."

She grins. "Maybe."

Lucy avoids the waves, and scrambles in the sand near Jennifer and me. The water slaps gently against the shore, and the sound is infinitely soothing. "This looks like a good place to come and wash away your troubles," I say.

"It is. Puget Sound is much mellower than the ocean." Jennifer gestures toward a large boat in the water. "Although in a few minutes, after that steamer passes, we'll get hit with some pretty massive waves, so you'll get a taste of what the ocean is like."

We stand around, watching dogs, and Jennifer says, "You should go check out the people beach. I'll be here for a while with these two."

"Okay." I trek back through the parking lot and make my way down toward the other side, staggering over several felled trees and large branches. The giant logs remind me of the trees that fell during a massive storm in Rooster last summer. The day I met Shelly. Downed trees closed roads and severed power for days, so when we both started our community service at the high school, we worked in the dark. With no air-conditioning, it was hotter than Satan's nuts inside the building.

The water beckons, and I remove my shoes and socks and set them on the sand. Being here reminds me of the day Theo took me to Richmond Beach. Back when I believed he and I were friends.

Reminder to self: don't agree to stay with your girlfriend's ex and not expect something bad to happen.

I stand with my toes glued to the sand and close my eyes, listening to seagulls whine as the water slaps against the beach. Soon, as Jennifer had warned, the surf roils and crashes against the shore, and my body thrums with a new intensity.

The poet Pablo Neruda said he needed the sea because each wave taught him something new. Maybe the key to understanding my father lies in a conversation with the sea. If I learn the language of the ocean, translate its hiss and vowels and rhythms, maybe then he and I can truly speak to one another.

Chapter Six

After dinner, Jennifer settles in with a book. I tell her I'm heading out. She offers her car, but sometimes it's easier to take the bus.

I head to Emerald City Books in Wallingford. Last time I was here I came with friends from the workshop. Like all the bookstores in town, they carry multiple copies of my father's new book.

In the café, I order a small coffee and sit at an outside table. I pull out my notebook and reread a story I started writing for Theo's class before I stopped attending. The story sucks, of course, and I'm crossing passages out when a girl waves a broom, and asks, "Can I steal your dirt?"

The words don't register right away until I realize she wants to sweep under my table. "Oh, sure." I lift my feet and she brushes the broom back and forth under me.

"Thanks."

"No problem. You can steal my dirt anytime."

"Too bad I don't work in a jewelry store," the girl says, as she sweeps the empty table next to mine. "I'd be able to sweep up diamonds that fell on the floor."

I laugh. She's not the kind of girl I'd notice right away, short, dark, and curvy, but she has a great smile. "I'm going to steal that line for what I'm writing." I write it in my notebook.

She glances over my shoulder. "You call me The Dirt Thief. I like it."

"It will be the story of a girl who steals dirt from a jewelry store. But the dirt turns into diamonds in her hands."

"Very clever. So, you're a writer."

"Allegedly."

"Seattle needs more writers," she says.

It takes me a second to realize she's being facetious. "I don't live here. I mean, I do for now, but I'm not sure for how long."

She nods and leans on the broomstick. "You know, the dirt thief could have several connotations. Literally, I stole the dirt from under your feet, but on a figurative level, one could steal "dirt," as in stories about them."

"But you have no dirt on me," I say. "You don't even know me."

She flaps her hands. "Then I'll make something up."

I wince. "I'm not sure which is worse, my truth or my fiction."

"What's your story?" she asks.

I strike a regal pose. "In my fictional tale, I'm a prince who owns a yacht, a private plane, and a small country." My shoulders sag. "In truth, I'm a wreck of a human being who can't finish a thought."

She belts out a hearty laugh, sets her broom aside, and sits across from me.

"Won't you get fired for loitering?"

She waves it off. "My uncle owns the cafe. My dad would kill him if he fired me."

I point my pen at her. "So, what's the dirt on *you*?"

"I'm a coffee shop waitress who sometimes chats with random strangers." She looks at my open notebook. "But it looks like I'm interrupting your work." She stands.

"I don't mind."

"I should get back to *my* work." She grabs her broom.

"Have fun while you're here."

"Thanks. And thanks for stealing my dirt."

"I'm going to sift through it and search for spare words. If I find any gems, I'll save them for you." She smiles and walks back inside the store.

I write down her exit line and mull it over. The Dirt Thief. What a great title, and as she pointed out, it contains a double entendre. Maybe I *will* write that story.

Chapter Seven

After my morning run and shower, I count through the rest of the bills in my wallet. My cash is almost gone, so if I decide to stay here permanently, I'll need a job. But I have enough money to buy a paperback and a cup of coffee at Emerald City Books.

Jennifer sits in the living room next to the fireplace reading, Lucy on her lap, Jack at her feet.

"The picture of domesticity," I say. "What are you reading?"

She holds up the book cover. "*All the Light We Cannot See*, by Anthony Doerr. It's for my book club."

"What's it about?"

She places the book face down on the table and clasps both hands over her heart. "It's a beautiful story of a blind French girl and a German boy in occupied France during World War Two."

"What do you like best about it?"

"The language is wonderful, almost like reading an epic poem."

"Sounds good. I'd like to read it."

"I'll loan it to you after tonight's discussion. I need to finish it before six, so I thought I'd read a couple of chapters before attacking the weeds in the back yard."

"I'll help you with the weeds when I get back. I'm headed to Emerald City Books."

She opens her book. "My keys are on the kitchen counter."

I hitch my bag over my shoulder. "Thanks, but I'll take the bus again."

My official reason to venture to Emerald City is to buy a Neruda, but the underlying reason is to see if the broom girl's there. I want to show her my story.

I hop off the bus and walk the two blocks to the bookstore.

The waitress isn't there, so I buy a cup of coffee and browse. I wander around the shelves, where I find a used copy of Neruda's *Selected Poems*. As if on cue, it falls open to the poem, *Ode to a Tomato*. Images of Shelly and me sharing a ripe tomato stream through my head. It was Saturday, a few days after we met. The building was closed, and we didn't have to report on weekends, but she showed up at the school, knowing I'd be there because I was still living in The Whale. I often parked my car in a shady spot near the football field.

The day was hot, so after I cashed my paycheck, we took a drive out in the middle of nowhere where it was cooler. Shelly and I bought fruit and tomatoes at a farm stand. As I drove along the narrow, winding road she held up a sweet, ripe tomato for me to bite into. I didn't mind that its juice dribbled down my chin. I hadn't even kissed her yet, but even then, I knew Shelly was someone special.

I thumb through the Neruda to find a poem that won't remind me of Shelly. But every Neruda poem reminds me of her. She nicknamed me Neruda. It's the name she gave me on my fake ID, making me twenty-two-year-old Michael F. Neruda.

I turn the page to *Ode to a Book*. There's something holy about words printed on paper, a miracle of infinite combinations of letters strung together to tell stories and supply information. Yet books also make me think of Shelly.

On page 359, the poem called *Fear* reads as if Neruda channeled my life story.

No poem is safe for me, but I buy the book anyway.

After I pay for my paperback, I spot the girl with the broom standing in the restaurant. She sees me and waves. I wave in return and saunter over to the cafe.

"The writer," she says.

"One of the many here in Seattle."

She smiles at me. "Are you coming in or leaving?"

I wave my empty cup. "I could stay for another cup of coffee."

She picks up a menu and escorts me to a table by the window. "How is the Dirt Thief coming along?"

I pull the story out of my bag and slide it across the table toward her. "It's still in draft, but I brought you a copy."

She claps her hands. "Oh, this is exciting. I can't wait to read it."

"Even if it portrays you as a knife wielding, mass murderer?"

"*Especially* if it does."

Now I feel obligated to order food, so I look over the menu and ask what she recommends for a light snack.

"Well, today we have *galaktompoureko*."

"Sounds like a contagious disease."

Laura Moe

She laughs. "It's wonderful. Kind of like a cross between custard and *baklava.*"

I raise my eyebrows, and say, "You may as well be speaking Greek."

She rolls her eyes. "It *is* Greek. You've never tried *baklava?*"

"I'm from Rooster, Ohio."

"Do you like cheesecake?" I nod. She takes the menu and taps me on the arm. "Trust me, you'll love it."

As she turns to walk off, I say, "Hey, did you find any diamonds in my dirt?"

"As a matter of fact, I did." She winks, and strides to the kitchen.

I still don't know her name. Is it too late to ask? She hasn't asked my name, either. Shelly would know the protocol, but I can't ask *her.*

The waitress comes back with my refilled coffee cup and sets a plate in front of me. I look for a name tag, but don't linger too long in case she thinks I'm scoping out her large boobs. "It *looks* like cheesecake."

"It's so much better than cheesecake."

I lift my fork and take a bite and all the seasons melt inside my mouth. "I think this may be the best thing I've ever tasted."

"It's the food of the gods," she says. "How will you describe it when you return to Ohio?"

"After this I may never go back." I take another bite, and let the flavors assimilate on my tongue. "It has the zesty citrus of summer, the warmth of autumn, yet the density of winter."

She smiles at me. "You really are a writer."

"What's your name?" I ask.

She sits across from me at the table. "Persephone Alexandria Diamandis. But everyone calls me Peri."

"The goddess of spring."

"Do you know Greek mythology?"

"A little. I had a Mythology class when I was a sophomore." I extend my hand. "My name's Michael Flynn. No relation to the bad guy who sold us to the Russians."

Peri grins. "You could change it."

"I'm kind of used to it."

"Do you have a nickname?".

"The only nickname I've ever had was Flynnstone. And my..." I was about to say girlfriend, but I amend it. "A friend of mine calls me Neruda."

Peri glances at my book. "Because you're a poet?"

"More that I just like his work."

Peri leans toward me. "I have a confession to make. I saw you in the store earlier, and I was going to come over and say hello, but you seemed upset."

I look down and fill my mouth with more pastry.

"I know it's none of my business, but I hope you feel better now," she adds.

I wipe my mouth with the napkin. "It was a poem I was reading. The language was so wonderful." She doesn't need to know the ten thousand other levels of grief I suffer.

She lifts my fork and takes a bite of the unpronounceable dessert. "So how come you're in Seattle?"

"I came for two things: to take a writing workshop and to meet my father."

"Wow. Two life changing events. How has your life changed?"

I slurp some coffee as I contemplate a reply. "In some ways it's better, and in other ways it's worse."

"Intriguing." She sets down the fork. "I like you Michael Flynnstone Neruda. I'm going to let you ask me out for a date." She eyes me. "That is, if you don't already have a girlfriend."

I take back my fork and shovel in another bite. "First, you have to tell me about the diamonds you found."

"I'm looking at a very rough one right now."

Chapter Eight

Jennifer's friend picks her up around 6:30 for book club. A few minutes later, I snatch her car keys and back the Camry out of the garage. The radio is set to a jazz station, but I'm curious about what other stations Seattle listens to. All we have back in Rooster are country, rock, and oldies. A few Columbus stations sputter in, but there's more static than music. I hit the scan arrow and hear snatches of classical, more jazz, talk, more talk, rock, Christian rock, Spanish talk radio, hard rock, and Indian. I push 'set' to listen to the Indian music. It sounds both awful and mesmerizing. I wonder if it'll grow on me.

I tell Jennifer's navigation system to guide me to Elliot Bay Books. It points me toward I-5 and I head south.

Even though rush hour ended long ago, traffic in Seattle is heavy. Eventually, I exit on Stewart Street, follow the GPS's directions, and park in a lot near the store.

A large sign advertising tonight's poetry reading hangs near the front window. I saunter into the coffee shop and order a small *cafe Americano*. As I descend the stairs for the reading, I'm drawn in by a female voice as she utters, "...names are like houses, small portraits of you under glass, hung in different rooms, rooms that have scarred walls, as if history mutates, wrinkles the map, and the mapmaker omits a town, that funky little town with a lonely strip motel off Highway Four near Otis, Kansas, its sputtering neon sign missing the *T*, a place where the price of checking in is miles and miles of open spaces."

Laura Moe

I sit in the back row in one of the folding chairs and set the coffee cup near my feet. The poet seems familiar. Then it hits me; she's Theo's friend Flora. My stomach clenches. I scan the room and recognize the back of the two-faced-lying-rat-bastard's head sitting in the front row, his arm draped casually over the adjacent chair.

Shit. I want to hear more of Flora's work, but I don't relish an encounter with Theo. I gulp my coffee down and slip upstairs after she finishes another poem.

Seeing him sours my mood, and I don't even want to scan the shelves, so I head to the parking lot.

The summer evening is balmy, and Jennifer's spaceship of a car will take me anywhere I desire, but I head back to my father's house. A long thumping beat with an occasional wail from a sitar accompanies me through the mass of cars on the freeway to the 85th Street exit. The music is growing on me.

Before shutting off the ignition, I change the radio back to jazz. At the side door, Jack greets me first, followed by Lucy.

I retrieve the book I bought the other day at Barnes and Noble and the dogs and I venture to the back yard. There's an hour or so of enough light left to read.

Jack and Lucy occupy each other with the dog bones strewn across the yard as I sink into a yellow Adirondack chair. I prop my bare feet on the opposite chair and crack open *Ron Carlson Writes a Story*. In the book the author describes how he forms a story called, "The Governor's Ball."

64

The author writes about a time he and his son wandered in the woods, and the son says, "Don't you love it when you don't know where you're going?"

Life's kind of like that. Every day adds more layers to my story and I never know what will happen next. Like tonight. I had no idea I'd see Theo. If someone told me ahead of time he'd be there, I would have chosen a different bookstore. There are tons of them in Seattle.

Was I *meant* to see him? Was this the part of my personal story arc where I need Theo to remind me of Shelly? But everything reminds me of Shelly.

Jack and Lucy suddenly become alert, and Jack scuttles to the French doors leading to the kitchen. My father stands there, looking at me. His expression is unreadable—not unfriendly—yet not welcoming, as if he's forgotten I'm staying here. He leans down, scratches Jack's fur, and asks, "Where's Jenny?"

"Book club."

He nods. "I came back a day early. I'll text her to let her know." He and Jack retreat inside the house.

Lucy remains under my feet, and she and I stay outside until it grows too dark to read.

My father sits at the breakfast bar, a glass of white wine and a stack of mail next to him. He's freshly showered, his damp hair combed back from his forehead. He's wearing his wedding band.

"How was Pacific Beach?"

"Cold." He grabs his dog's snout. "I should have taken my buddy here to keep me warm."

"Jennifer and I took the dogs to the dog beach yesterday. Jack's a good swimmer."

"He loves the water."

The front door opens, and Lucy skitters to greet Jennifer. "Hi, sweet pea," I hear from the hallway. She enters the kitchen holding an empty fruit bowl. "Hey, handsome." She kisses my father and strokes his gritty chin with the back of her hand. "Come here often?" She sets the fruit bowl in the sink.

"As often as I can." He lifts his wine. "Should I pour you a glass?"

"No, I had plenty at book club tonight. What brings you home early?"

"Brian's wife started having labor pains."

Jennifer looks over at me. "Brian is one of Ash's colleagues." She drapes herself across my father's shoulders. "Did you get enough samples?"

"More than enough. Had a good team with us this time." He slips his arm around her waist and pulls her against him. "What did you do while I was away?"

She steals a sip of his wine. "Michael and I walked Green Lake, bought some plants at Sky Nursery, and took the dogs to Marina Beach." She looks at me. "What else did we do?"

"You finished your smutty book."

My father raises his eyebrows. "Smutty book?"

"She's reading *Fifty Shades of Grey*," I say.

Jennifer shrugs. "I need to learn what to do with all those whips and chains in the closet."

My father sniggers and refills his wine glass.

"Speaking of books." Jennifer pulls a blue hardback out of her bag and hands it to me. "We had the best discussion about this tonight and I'm curious to see what you think."

"Thanks." I glance at the inside flap and set it on top of the Ron Carlson.

"Is that the smutty book?" my father asked.

"No, *that* one is on the bedside table." She wraps her arms around him again and squeezes. "Mmmmmmmm. I'm glad you're home."

He rests his face against hers. "It's good to be home."

Once again, I'm the third wheel. "I think I'll go up and start reading. Good night." I grab both books and take two steps at a time to the attic bedroom.

Chapter Nine

Peri's back is to me as she waits on a table for two, her thick, wavy hair dangling in an unruly braid halfway down her back. Her apron is tied loosely around her wide hips, and she chats with a pair of customers. I slink into a chair at the next table and dump my bag on the adjacent seat.

She finishes taking the couple's order and turns to greet me, setting down a menu before looking at my face.

"Oh! It's you!"

"It is I."

"How are you?"

"Good."

"I loved the story you wrote about me."

The man at the next table turns, and says, "Miss, could you save your flirting for another time and bring our coffees, please?"

"She wasn't flirting," I say. I want to kick the asshole in the nuts.

Peri gives me a dismissive wave, and whispers, "It's okay." To the asshole, she says sweetly, "I'll be right back with those, sir." She disappears behind the counter and I give him the stink eye, but he goes back to reading his *New York Times.*

A couple of minutes later Peri sets two frothy coffee drinks in front of the couple. "Is there anything else I can bring you?"

"This is fine, thank you," says the woman. She has shoulder-length red hair and a buttery voice.

Peri steps away, but the man sips his drink, and shoves the cup to the edge of the table. "It's cold."

"Oh," Peri says. "I'm sorry."

"The whipped cream is cold, honey," the redhead tells him. "Just stir it into the drink."

"I didn't order whipped cream. Bring me one without it."

"Sure." Peri whisks his cup away.

I arch towards them. "It's not her fault, so I hope this doesn't affect her tip."

"Nobody asked your opinion," the man snaps.

"Gary, please. Can we just relax and have a cup of coffee?"

"As long as this jerk minds his own damned business."

"Fuck you," I mutter. I know this will end badly if I keep sitting here. I text Peri. *-Want to kill the asshole @next table. Going inside bookstore. Txt when u get a chance.*

P-Off in 30 min. Can u wait?

-Duh. In a bookstore. Will be here for days.

-☺

In the fiction section I jot down a few interesting titles, hoping Jennifer might have them at home.

Home is a curious word for a place where I feel like an interloper. Even though Earl and Dot are not blood, I feel more 'at home' at their farm than I do inside my mother's trashy house full of broken junk or my father's well-maintained house full of books.

What made me stay here after the workshop ended? All those stupid movies rolling in my head about fathers and sons bonding and shit? The Hollywood ending isn't written into my script. It hasn't been a horror film, but it's not a heartwarming Hallmark saga, either.

What *did* I expect? This guy doesn't know me from the man on the moon. Maybe Shelly's lucky she never found her real mother. The truth can hurt, and the truth is my father doesn't like me. And why should he? I've got nothing to offer the Dr. Oz of oceanography.

Maybe I should have gone home. I don't belong here.

Yet I do. Seattle fits me. My father may not want me, but Seattle does. The city flaunts its wares at me like a carnival barker. *You want bookstores, coffee shops, libraries, universities, ferries, trains, buses, people speaking a litany of incomprehensible languages, opera on stage, jazz in the street, foods you can't pronounce? We got that here, kid.*

I feel a feminine hand on my back and turn to see Peri. "Sorry I ran out," I say. "I was ready to flatten that guy."

"It's okay. I wasn't expecting you in the first place."

"Did the asshole leave a tip?"

"His wife hid a couple of bucks under her cup."

"Seems like nice women always end up with assholes."

She shoulder-bumps me. "I guess I'd better sharpen my claws."

"I'm sorry I didn't return your text last night."

"I'll forgive you this time."

One of her springy curls dangles near her face and I loop it in my index finger. "You deserve someone with better manners than me."

"You're not the worst person I've ever met." She hikes her bag over her shoulder. "Want to go for a walk?"

"Sure."

We set out on the street. As we stroll, I say, "I was hesitant to text back because I just broke up with someone, and I don't know what I'm doing here."

"I'm sorry."

"I'm probably terrible dating material."

"Who said anything about dating?" she says. "We can just be friends, you know."

I look over at her. "I've never had a girl as a friend before. I mean, Shelly and I were friends at first, I guess...I don't know what I'm saying."

"Breakups are tough. They fry your brain cells." She takes my free hand. Having a girl's soft fingers in mine improves the day. "Tell me how things are going with your father."

I shrug. "His wife Jennifer and I get along great."

"That's not what I asked."

I release her hand and punch the button for the crosswalk. I scrunch my face and look up, as if the words I need are written in the sky. "Jennifer says to give it time."

The light changes, and I retrieve Peri's hand as we cross the street. On the other side, she gazes up at me. "You've had a bad few weeks, haven't you, Michael?"

"It's like I sneezed, but there's no one around to bless me."

She wraps her hands around my arm, something Shelly used to do, yet my muscles feel the difference. "I know something that will make you feel better about life."

My eyebrows shoot up. "Sex? Drugs? Rock and roll?"

"Better. Trust me." She pulls me down the block and guides me inside a dingy coffee shop. "They have the most delectable chocolate-covered-chocolate cupcakes in the Pacific Northwest.".

I scan the price board. The cupcakes are three seventy-five and a small coffee is three bucks. I pull my wallet out, but Peri stops me. "My treat."

Peri suggests I get a cinnamon chai latte and the chocolate cupcake. She orders the same, and we carry our goodies to a small table near the back. "This cupcake is enormous. Good thing I ran this morning."

"Calories don't count when you're sad," she says.

"Am I sad?"

"You like to hide it, but yes, you're sad."

I bite a chunk from the side of the cupcake and end up with chocolate frosting on my nose. My eyes are slivers as I savor the flavor.

"Told you this would make you feel better about life."

I lick my lips, wipe the frosting off my nose, and suck more frosting off my fingers.

"Now take a drink of the chai."

I do, and the flavors mingle. "You have led me down the path of addiction."

Peri hands me a napkin. "What happened with your girlfriend?"

I wipe my lips and spill the whole sordid tale.

***

When I finish, Peri says, "wow, that's quite a story."

"You don't know the half of it." I reveal the rest of my tale of having a succession of stepfathers, my mother's hoarding, and living in my car. "I wish none of it were true."

She touches my hand. "But think of the great stories you can tell your grandchildren."

I huff. "Hopefully by then I'll have my shit together."

"How old *are* you?"

"Nineteen."

"You're pretty interesting for someone so young."

"How old are *you*?"

"Twenty-two," she says.

I show her Michael Neruda's ID. "I'm the same age."

She laughs. "Your life between now and the age your fake driver's license says you are will change exponentially. You'll look back at your nineteen-year-old self and wonder 'what was that guy's problem?'"

"What changes?"

"You get less wrapped up in trivial stuff. Like that jerk who didn't want whipped cream on his latte. At nineteen, he would have had me in tears. But after living on my own in Chicago, I realized it wasn't about me. It was latte guy's problem."

We take the bus over to Green Lake to walk off our cupcakes. I take her hand in mine and we begin the three-mile trek around the lake. Peri's fingers are tiny, almost like a child's, yet I don't feel the need to protect Peri from herself as I did when I was with Shelly.

A mile into our walk, I point out my father's house.

Peri's eyes grow big. "Wow. You guys have some money."

"He does. I don't."

We move on and spot a guy sitting on a bench with a portable typewriter in his lap. A sign next to him reads, HELP ME WRITE MY WAY ACROSS THE COUNTRY. POEMS or STORIES ON DEMAND $5.

"What's the deal?" I ask him. "I give you five bucks and you create a poem or story for me?"

"That's it," the guy says. He's wearing a UW ball cap and the scruff of someone who spends his nights in a tent city.

I glance at Peri. She nods, and I say, "Okay, how about a poem?"

"Tell me a theme or element you want to include," the storyteller says.

"How about...my life is just one damn thing after another."

"Okay. Is this for you or her?"

"You choose," I say.

The storyteller inserts a piece of paper into the machine and starts typing. Peri pulls a sketch pad and a pencil out of her bag and sketches the man as he writes.

After a few minutes, he rolls the paper out of his typewriter and hands the sheet to me.

Oh, The Trouble I've seen
I wish I could write you a song
But I can't sing a note.
Even if I sang it
All my guitar strings broke
and there's a hole

in my pocket where my wallet should be.
If I wrote you that song it
Would be the worst country song on the radio
and listeners would call and complain.
But my song is really the blues.
Oh, the trouble I've seen.
By the end of the day
You will wish you'd never asked how I was today.
by Eric Evans

Peri reads over my shoulder and she and I laugh together.

"This is perfect." I pay the guy and fold the poem in between the pages of my journal book. "How long have you been doing this?"

"A couple of years," Eric says. "

"Do you like writing on demand?"

He considers this for a second. "Most of the time."

"Good luck to you."

We continue our stroll and Peri looks up at me. "Do you feel better about life, now?"

I retrieve her hand. "I do. Thanks."

It's a bright day at the lake, and we're surrounded by strangers, yet connected by a need to feed our bodies and souls with fresh air. This happens everywhere, even in Rooster, Ohio.

Shelly always knocks living in our nothing town, but parts of it are exquisite. She didn't spend rainy days playing in the mud on summer evenings, catching lightning bugs in a jar. She doesn't know the simple pleasures poor children explore, like lying on the grass to watch the clouds converse, chasing your brother through corn fields where the stalks loom above your heads, or finding treasures inside abandoned houses.

We walk to Peri's house and are greeted by an enormous, furry brown and tan cat. "This is Pooh Kitty."

I lean down to pet him, but he slinks away.

Peri opens her front door. "Come in and meet my parents."

In the kitchen, a middle-aged dark-haired man sits across the table from a voluptuous redhead. They're playing a card game and both look up when Peri and I walk in.

"What are you playing?" Peri asks.

Her mother sets her cards face down on the table. "I have no idea. It's something your father made up."

"It's two-person solitaire," Peri's dad says.

Mrs. Diamandis wears an exasperated expression. "I keep telling him the whole point of *soli*taire is you can play it alone. That's why it's called *soli*taire."

Her father shrugs and collects the cards. He looks up at me. "Who's this guy?"

"Mom, Dad, this is my friend Michael."

Her mother claps her hands. "The writer!"

I shoot Peri a look. "They read your story."

Peri's mother grabs my hand. "We're very nosy about who our children spend time with." She studies me. "You're good-looking, but way too thin."

"Mom!"

"I run a lot," I say.

"You should also remember to eat."

Peri pours herself a glass of water from the tap. "Believe me, Mom, he eats like a stevedore."

Her mother stands up and goes to the fridge. "I have something I want you to try." She pulls out a small aluminum pan and slides the pan into the toaster oven.

"Mom, is that leftover *tiropita?*"

Mrs. Diamandis glances at me. "You're going to love this, Michael."

"It's fantastic," Peri says. She fixes us each a glass of iced tea.

Her father clears space at the table. "Peri said you came here from Ohio."

I give them the brief run-down of attending the workshop. A savory aroma envelops us, and shortly the kitchen timer bings. Peri's mother slices four wedges of pastry and sets them on small plates. She hands us each a fork and a plate.

"What am I eating?" I ask.

"*Tiropita.* It's a cheese pie made with phylo dough and feta and topped with butter."

"Man, this *is* good," I say.

After we finish eating, I thank the Diamandises for the snack and Peri whisks me up toward her room. When we reach the middle stair, Mrs. Diamandis yells from the kitchen, "Leave the door open."

"Seriously, Mom? I'm a college graduate."

"You know the rules, young lady."

"Oh-*kay.*" She sighs, and guides me into her room. "Welcome to my little shop of horrors."

I haven't been in many girls' rooms, but Peri's looks more like an art gallery than a bedroom. On the wall opposite her bed hang black and white enlargements of portraits. I walk over to take a closer look.

Some of the pictures reveal people sleeping on sidewalks and benches, loosely swaddled in layers of dirty blankets and torn overcoats. Others are close-ups of faces ravaged from drugs, alcohol, and hard living, yet I recognize a hollow beauty in the faces of these men and women.

"I call these my experiments with ugliness," she says.

"They're extraordinary. You captured their resigned desperation." I do a quick scan of the photos again. "Most of these are taken at night. Did you go there after dark?"

"My brother Alex was with me." She plops on the bed and sits cross legged. "He's a sociology major at U- dub. He had an assignment to spend twenty-four hours among the homeless." She rubs her feet. "I was interested, so I asked if I could go with him. I brought along my sketch book and camera."

"How did you convince people to let you take their picture?"

"Amazing what a sandwich or a couple of bucks will give you access to."

"That's true. Back when I lived in my car Shelly bought me breakfast every day, and she gained access to my body and soul."

The opposite wall is covered in nudes: full frontal, full back, partial, male and female. Some are drawn in charcoal or pencil, others in pastel and paint. "You're really good."

"Thanks. Figure drawing is my favorite class."

I smirk. "Is that because you get to look at naked people all day?"

She sputters a laugh. "When I'm drawing, I just see them as shapes and shadows, not boobs and wieners."

Chapter Ten

Fog surrounds the lake this morning as I run. My phone rings. I slow my pace, pull my phone out of my arm band, and see it's Peri. "Hey."

"Hi. Why do you sound like an obscene phone caller? I wheeze out a chuckle. "I'm running around the lake." I shift the phone to my other ear.

"What are you up to?"

"Working on a drawing."

"Of someone naked?"

"Naturally," she says. "I have a crowd of naked men in my bedroom posing for me."

"I take it your mom isn't home."

Peri laughs. "She's at work. So, what's it like to run in the fog?"

"Like running any day except you can't see much."

"Narrate it as if you were writing a story."

"My writing muscles have gotten flabby," I say.

"Try it."

I groan. "Fog hovers over the water like a gloved hand, and shadows of people creep along its edges."

"Nice! See? You've still got it."

"Barely. Hey, are you working today?"

"Nope. Once I send all the naked men home, I'm free the rest of the day."

"Want to get together? I was going to check out Half Price Books in Lynnwood. Or maybe you can corrupt me with more sinful food and beverages."

"Sure. Whatever."

"I'll text you after I clean up."

I finish my run and head back to the house for a shower. I dress and go downstairs. Lucy and Jack's Cat chase one another in the back yard as Jennifer tends to her vegetable patch. Jack reclines in a sunny spot nearby.

"I thought I'd check out Half Price Books with my friend Peri," I say. "Do you mind if I borrow your car?"

She turns and squints at me from under her gardening hat. "I'm glad you have at least one friend here. I was starting to think you'd star in *Friendless in Seattle*."

"Ha ha." I give her a crooked grin and kneel down next to her.

She wipes her brow with the back of her hand. "The car is yours for as long as you need it. I plan to just garden and read today."

"Thanks. Hey, I started reading *All the Light We Cannot See*. Anthony Doerr is a damn good writer."

"I'm anxious to hear what you think when you're done." She pulls off her gardening gloves. "Do I get to meet this Perry?"

"Maybe."

Jennifer stands and dusts the grass off her knees. "Ask him to come over for dinner."

"Peri's a girl. I met her at Emerald City Books."

She snaps her fingers. "Speaking of books, I have some to give you."

I follow her back into the house. She goes into her study and comes back holding a Trader Joe's sack filled with books and DVDs. "Sell whatever you don't want at Half Price Books and keep the money. Or take your friend Peri out to lunch."

"Thanks. I could use some cash."

"Any time you need money, just ask."

I grimace. "If I decide to stay here I should get a job before asking for handouts."

Peri's house isn't far, and she's standing in her front yard as I pull into her driveway. As usual, she carries her enormous shoulder bag. "Nice wheels."

"If I didn't like my father's wife so much, I'd steal it."

This time of day traffic is light, so we make it to Lynnwood in less than fifteen minutes. Peri and I walk to the buy-back area at Half Price Books where I set the bag on the counter. The clerk asks if I've sold items with them before.

"Not at this one."

She requests my driver's license, and I hand her my real one.

"Ohio," she says. "You came a long way to sell books." She types in my license number and hands it back to me. "Okay, Michael, give us about twenty minutes. There's a couple people ahead of you."

When I turn, I bump into a tall, rangy-looking guy with a ponytail. "Dale!"

"Hey, you're still in town. How's it going?" He dumps his bags on the floor and throws his arms around me in a bear hug.

I wonder how much Theo's roommate knows about our falling out. I'm pretty sure Dale heard the scuffle. "I'm staying with my father for a while." I gesture to Peri and introduce them to each other. "Are you still working the night security job?"

"I've moved on to working as a custodian at the university," he says.

I tell Peri, "Dale is intentionally working a succession of blue collar jobs to understand their effects on the writing process. He's documenting the experiences for his doctoral dissertation."

"Some of our finest writers worked mind-numbing jobs," he says. "Jack Kerouac, Li Young Lee, Jim Daniels, Irene McInerny. My theory is that the mind-numbing work provides a blank canvas upon which to formulate great ideas."

"Does the work help *you* write?" Peri asks.

Dale considers this for a second. "It does. This is kind of like immersion research that pays pretty well."

"Do they have any openings?" I ask.

"They might. They've outsourced dorm cleaning to a private company that may need workers. Why? You interested?"

"I have some actual custodial experience."

He reaches for his phone and hands it to me. "Type in your number in and I'll find out." He types his digits into my phone, too. "I'll be in touch."

I clap his shoulder. "It was good seeing you, Dale."

"Good seeing you, too. Hey, do you know how trash collectors get trained?" he asks.

"No."

"They pick it up as they go along."

I groan. "Always good talking to you, Dale."

As we walk away, Peri asks softly, "How do you know that guy?"

"I'll explain later."

We roam around the store until Peri finds the art books. She picks out a book on how to draw hands. Then we head for the Language Arts section. I stop in front of the dictionaries and thesauruses and swipe a finger across the bindings. "When my old frenemy Rick and I were library aides in middle school, he and I would smack each other with the reference books as we shelved them. We called it The Attack of the Thesauri."

"Is this the guy whose car you tried to blow up?"

"Yeah."

"I'll bet your librarian loved it."

"Mrs. Morgan would just put her hands on her hips and shake her head." I pull a Webster's thesaurus off the shelf. "Did you know there's no synonym for thesaurus? The dictionary calls it a dictionary of related words."

"I always thought it was for finding a word to replace one you can't spell."

"That's why *I* use it."

She laughs.

I pull a large American Heritage Dictionary down and thumb through it. "I have a confession to make. And it may change the way you feel about me."

"Oh?"

I slide the book back in its place, hang my head, and utter in a low voice, "I carry a thesaurus with me at all times."

She feigns shock and grips her chest as if she's been stabbed. "Oh my god!"

I alter my voice to a whisper. "It's a battered paperback with yellowed pages. The spine is cracked in three places and JOE is scrawled across the cover in black marker."

"It sounds like a priceless collector's item."

"I bought it for two reasons: one, it was only a dollar, and two, I wondered which words Joe liked best."

"What are his favorites?"

I think for a second. "He'd underlined *coincident* and *equivalent*, *disorder* and *inoculate*. He also dog-eared the page with the synonyms for sex."

"What a disorderly coincidence."

I glance back at my pack. "I have another confession. I also carry a dictionary."

"You are one sick puppy."

"True. But you never know when you might have a word emergency."

"How come you don't just use the app on your phone?"

I sniff as if offended. "The app only skims the surface of a word's etymology."

She makes a gagging motion. "Word nerd."

I point to her bag. "Art nerd. You're always packing art supplies. And possibly a refrigerator."

She giggles. "No, just a toaster oven."

My name is called on the loudspeaker and she and I walk back to the buy-back area. Jennifer's books and DVDs score me $16.50.

I pocket my money. "Do you want to go to Starbucks across the street? My treat."

"You mean charbucks?"

"Yeah, I know. Their coffee tastes burnt, but I still have a few bucks left on my Starbucks card. And it's close by."

She orders a chocolate croissant and an *Americano*. I splurge and buy myself a *venti* mocha latte and a brownie. We sit at a shady table outside.

She brushes some of her springy hair away from her face and gathers her thick curls into a single ponytail. "Are you planning to stay in town for good?"

"I'm still not sure." I take a slurp of my latte. "If I go back to Ohio, I have a free ride at a local college for two years. But my father can help me go to UW for practically nothing." I dunk my brownie in my cup.

Peri nibbles on her croissant and wipes her fingers with one of the thin napkins. "There's no hurry. You only need to decide your future last week."

I bark a laugh. "I do my best work making 'seat-of-my-pants' decisions."

She sips her *Americano*. "Sometimes we don't know what to do until we're faced with a deadline."

"Or we make poor choices." I swallow the last bite of my brownie and wipe my mouth. "Given my felonious background, will college even help keep me from living under a bridge?"

"I don't think they hold high school pranks against people forever. You won't be able to move to Canada, though."

"Why not?"

"They don't allow anyone in who's had a felony arrest."

I throw my hands in the air. "There goes my plan to join the Royal Canadian Mounties."

She grins. "Not to change the subject, but how do you know the guy in the bookstore?"

"Dale is Theo's roommate."

She raises her eyebrows. "Your friend Theo from the workshop?"

"My *ex*-friend."

"You seem to accumulate a lot of *ex*-friends."

"I don't mean to. It's just when I start to care about people they crap on my head."

She wraps her fingers around the base of her cup. "Don't take this the wrong way, but do you ever wonder if subconsciously, you let things like this happen?"

"I…"

"I'm not saying you deserve it, but that you *believe* you do."

I sit back and cross my arms. "I hadn't considered that."

She leans her elbows on the table and clasps her hands. "I've had a history of being dumped on by guys. Eventually I realized I allowed that to happen."

"Wow. Really?"

"The last guy I dated cheated on me, and I was so distraught, my roommate talked me into going to a therapist

Laura Moe

on campus." She pinches a few crumbs from her plate. "My therapist helped me see that, on a subconscious level, I believed I didn't deserve romantic love."

"Why?"

"I've always been self-conscious about my looks: big nose, big butt, big hair."

"You look pretty good to me."

She waves me away. "You didn't grow up being called Bubble Butt or Flippo the Clown because of your enormous butt and wild hair."

"I got called plenty of other names."

She plucks the lid off her cup and stirs her drink. "School is hell if you're the least bit different. But it gets better in college because everyone is starting with a clean slate."

"Except if I go back to Rooster, I'll be at a branch campus in the same city with the same people who know me from high school."

She places a hand over mine. "I've always had pretty good self-esteem. I know I'm intelligent, funny, and a good artist, but somewhere deep in my psyche I still believed I was undatable." She arcs closer to me at the table. "It was as if I sought out guys totally wrong for me, narcissistic bad boys who would be cruel and never love me back."

I pick at the lid on my cup. "Am I a narcissist?"

She scrunches her brow. "Not totally. You're self-centered, but that's because you need so much. But you also give back." She sips her coffee. "Anyway, I'm working on taking better control in my relationships."

88

"Does that mean you'll spend more time with me?"

She shrugs. "I like being around you. I think we make good friends."

"We do." I gulp the rest of my latte. "By the way, Jennifer wants me to invite you to dinner."

"Tonight?"

I raise my eyebrows. "I guess? I've never brought a girl home before so I don't know the protocol."

"Really? You never took a girl to your house?"

"My mother's house looks like it was hit by a missile. I was afraid someone might get sucked into a vortex of cataclysm."

She laughs. "Why don't you text your stepmother and ask her the proper protocol?"

***

The house oozes onions and red sauce. My father is right; Italian food does smell like heaven. Jack and Lucy bark their greetings and Peri stoops to pet them.

"We're in the kitchen," Jennifer yells.

My father holds a knife above a row of carrots.

"You're cooking again?" I ask.

He tilts his head toward Jennifer, stirring a pot on the stove. "After the spaghetti disaster, she put me on salads."

"You're not getting a permanent get-out-of-cooking-dinner card, though." Jennifer winks at me. "Only when we have guests." She rests the spoon on the stove, wipes her hands, and extends one toward Peri. "Hi. I'm Jennifer, and my salad chef is Ash."

Peri takes Jennifer's hand. "I'm Peri."

Jennifer looks at me. "It's another gorgeous night, so we're going to dine *al fresco* again. Will you set the table?"

I grab four plates and sets of silverware and the dogs follow me out to the back yard.

Peri comes out holding a pitcher of iced tea. "You didn't tell me your father is Dr. Ashton Meadows," she whispers.

"You know who he is?"

"*Everybody* knows who he is."

"Oh, right. He's the Dr. Oz of oceanography."

Peri and I make several trips in and out gathering glasses, bread, napkins, and platters of pasta in red sauce, and the salad. My father carries an open bottle of red and four wine glasses and sets them on the table. "Peri, do you drink wine?"

She smiles at him. "Occasionally."

"I think this is an occasion." He empties the bottle into four glasses and hands one to each of us.

We pull back our chairs and sit. Jennifer squeezes my father's hand. "The salad looks lovely, Honey Bear."

He wears a giant grin. "My salad is a masterpiece."

Peri giggles and eyes my father more closely. Her cheeks are flushed.

The four of us cut into our food and eat until Jennifer breaks the silence. "Michael says you work at Emerald City Books."

Peri swallows a bite of salad and chases it with a dab of wine. "For now. I just finished my BA at the Art Institute in Chicago."

"What do you plan to do with your degree?"

"I'm exploring getting my MFA at U dub."

"Ash teaches at the university," Jennifer says.

"I'm in the Biology department," he says.

"My husband is being modest. He's a world-renowned oceanographer, a bestselling author, and a hunk of burning love."

My father snickers and gulps some wine.

Peri gives the Dr. Oz of Oceanography a radiant smile.

My father reaches for Peri's left wrist and runs his thumb over her beaded bracelet. "I see you have a 4Ocean bracelet."

Peri looks down at her wrist. "Yes. My brother got us each one for Christmas last year."

"Those guys have done a bang-up job of cleaning up the ocean," he says.

"What are you talking about?" I ask.

My father lets go of Peri's wrist and his fingers sweep across her hand. "Two young surfers concocted a plan to clean up the ocean. They make the bracelets from recycled glass and plastics found in the sea. The proceeds go to fund further clean ups. So far, 4Ocean has cleaned up more than 300,000 pounds of debris."

"Oh." I only half listen because my father's hand is still touching Peri's.

He finally lifts his hand off hers and stabs at his salad. "Peri, tell us about your art work."

"I work in several media: photography, charcoal, oils."

"My wife is also an artist. Most of the paintings on our walls are hers."

"I'll have to take a look when we go back inside." Peri turns to Jennifer. "What's your favorite subject?"

"Whatever grabs my attention at the time," Jennifer replies. "How about you?"

Peri swirls her fork around a clump of noodles. "Lately I'm working on a series of people living in tent cities."

"Do you actually go to homeless camps?" Jennifer asks.

"Yes."

"Do you have any photos of your work?" My father asks.

Peri pulls her phone out of her pocket and opens her Instagram page. "I usually work with thirty-five millimeter, but I posted a few pics on Instagram." She passes her phone to my father. He sets his fork down and studies her Instagram feed. He squints at her. "How old are you?"

"Twenty-two."

"You have the eye of someone with a more mature view of the world." He passes the phone to Jennifer, who *oohs* and *aahs* at each picture she views.

Jennifer stops at one picture. "This guy looks familiar."

She turns the phone at me. The photo is a close up of me Peri took of me at the lake yesterday.

I narrow my eyes at Peri. "You included me in your homeless people portfolio?"

"Not intentionally." Peri takes her phone back and sets it face down on the table. "The picture just happens to be the last one I took."

"Uh huh." I wonder if Peri's interested in me as one of her subjects. Shelly collects naked men. Maybe Peri collects homeless dudes. But wait. I contacted *her.*

My father studies her. "What draws you to portraits?"

"Each face has a story to tell. They reflect a person's beauty, ugliness and pain. You can pile on the makeup and get an expensive haircut, but there's an energy behind one's face that can't be hidden. I like to discover what lies beneath."

My father nods and chews. "I feel the same way about ocean life. I'm drawn to the saga of sea."

"Ash likes turtles and fish better than people," Jennifer said.

He bumps his shoulder against Jennifer's. "I like you a tiny bit more." He pecks her cheek and looks back at Peri. "What have you discovered about humanity?"

Peri ponders this for a few seconds. "We're all bizarre creatures." She takes a bite of pasta. Her eyes are fixed on him as if they're on a date.

My father sets his fork down and steeples his hands. "Most of my work keeps me at sea level or a few feet below, but a few months ago I had the opportunity to participate with a team on a deep-sea dive to map the mid ocean ridge. Below us are depths greater than the Alps. I'd known this since my undergrad days, but to actually be there was life-changing."

"He writes about it in his new book," Jennifer says.

"Wow," Peri says. "How long were you there?"

"Most of last winter."

"He missed Christmas and New Year's," Jennifer says.

"Santa gifted me with layers of history, intrigue, danger, and drama seething below the ocean's surface." My father clasps his hands together and rests his elbows on the table. He gazes at Peri. "One little known fact is there are devastating earthquakes and volcanoes occurring underneath the ocean's surface."

"You mean earthquakes we can't feel?"

"Exactly. It's all part of the normal life cycle down below."

Peri twirls spaghetti over her fork but keeps her eyes locked on his. I resent the easy chemistry between them.

Jennifer tilts her head toward me, and mutters, "We may as well be invisible. Once he starts talking ocean stuff, he can go on for days."

As he speaks, my father's face is more animated than I've ever seen it. I need to learn the language of the ocean if he and I have any future.

Chapter Eleven

My father insists I use his car to drive Peri home rather than her taking the bus. As we head down Roosevelt, Peri says, "I like Jennifer and your dad."

"You and he seem to hit it off."

After a beat, she adds, "I think I have a little crush on him."

"You and ten thousand other women."

Her face breaks into a wide grin. "He's so smart. And he's kind of sexy."

I steal a glance at her. "What is it about him that makes women to go bat-shit crazy? Yeah, he's good looking and smart. Is it because he's semi-famous?"

"No. Fame doesn't make any difference to me."

"*I* look like him. And I have a bodacious vocabulary, yet women aren't knocking themselves out to be with me."

"Physically, you resemble him, but you have a different energy."

"What the hell does *that* mean?"

She considers this for a few seconds. "Well, your father has swagger."

"I don't have swagger?"

"I'm not saying you won't develop it, but…"

"But you're saying I'm not manly enough?"

"I didn't say that… it's just your father is very comfortable in his skin." She shrugs. "I don't know. There's just something about him."

Laura Moe

I pull up to a Stop sign. "Well, he doesn't do anything for me."

"That's because you're a guy."

I glance at her wrist. "Did you wear that bracelet just so my father would notice?"

"Are you kidding me? I've had this on since this morning, *before* you asked me to dinner. And I had no idea your father was Dr. Meadows." She studies me for a second. "Oh my God, you're jealous of your own father."

I drum my fingertips on the wheel. "He seems to get all the girls."

"He doesn't *have* me."

"But you admit you have a crush on him," I say.

"It's hard not to. He's a sexy guy who's trying to save the world."

I sputter a laugh. "Yeah, right. You just want to see him naked."

She swats me on the arm. "I wouldn't turn him down if he wanted to model for me. And his face has wonderful textures. The creases near his eyes, the stubble on his chin, and that messy hair. He's like a swashbuckler in an old black and white film."

I sneer.

"And he's so nice," she says.

I grunt. "Not to me, he isn't."

"You guys got along fine tonight."

"That's because you and Jennifer were there. He's only nice when there are women present. When *I'm* alone with him, it's like talking to a block of ice. And he watches me as if I'm planning to steal the silver."

"I'm sure you're exaggerating."

"The other night when we went out to dinner he practically choked to death when he had to introduce me to someone."

"At least he hasn't tossed you in the street."

I tense my jaw and turn onto a street a block away from Peri's. "Now might be a good time to change the subject."

"Okay," she says. "Tell me something good happening in your life."

I bark a laugh. "Nothing."

"Come on, Michael. Whining won't help you develop swagger."

I take a deep breath and exhale. "My friend Shoe is coming back to Seattle. I met him at the workshop."

"That's good since you're virtually friendless."

"Tell me about it."

"Why *are* you so unlikeable?"

"I don't know." I know she's kidding, but my own father doesn't like me. So maybe it *is* me. I pull up in front of her house and put the Subaru in park.

"You should come in and say hello."

I give her a side glance. "Aren't you afraid I'll fall hopelessly in love with your mother like you are with my father?"

She laughs. "She'd love that. Maybe a boy toy will get her out of her slump."

I shut off the car and release my seatbelt. "Why is she in a slump?"

Peri shrugs and opens her door. "She hates her job, but my parents can't afford for her to quit."

"So, two-person solitaire isn't paying off for your dad?"

"Hardly."

The inside of their home smells of chili and red pepper and I'm hungry again. Pooh Kitty greets us at the door, but swishes away from me when I reach down to pet him. In the kitchen Peri's mother is putting leftovers in the fridge. She turns, and says, "Michael. How nice to see you again."

"You're looking lovely tonight, Mrs. Diamandis."

Peri elbows me and grins. "Mom, we're heading up to my room."

"Leave the door open, honey."

Peri picks up the cat and carries him toward the steps. "Yes, Mom, I know."

With the door wide open we sit together on her bed. I peruse the life drawings on her wall. "You really are talented."

"Thanks." She leans on her elbows on the mattress like an easel. "I might have a job for you. I'm in a drawing group on Wednesdays and we're always looking for models."

"Naked?"

"You said you needed money. It pays well."

"How much?"

"Seventy-five bucks for three hours."

I sit on the bed next to her. "What would I have to do?"

She shrugs. "Just pose."

"For three hours?"

"We begin with short gesture poses, and then do a longer pose for two hours. But you get a break every half hour." She brushes cat hair off the bedspread. "The hardest part is just standing still."

"The hardest part would be if I got a boner."

"So far none of our men have done that."

I lie back on her bed. "How many people would be ogling my body?"

"Nine or ten. And there's nothing sexual about it. We're all artists who study the body for form."

"Hmmm." I squeeze my lips between two fingers. "I *have* posed nude before, even though I didn't know I did."

"You did?"

"When Shelly snapped the naked picture of me that her boy-toy threatened to put online."

Peri runs her hand over her bedspread. "It's up to you. We pay in cash."

"I could use the money."

She picks up her phone. "Should I let Dave know you're available if we need you?"

"This isn't some ploy to get me out of my boxers?"

She rolls her eyes. "You wish."

I flip onto my side and face her. "Sure. Why not? Maybe it'll help me develop some swagger."

Laura Moe

Chapter Twelve

All the Light We Cannot See keeps me up late, so it's after ten when I roll out of bed. Peri texts me to let me know they need a model today at one o'clock if I'm interested. I decide not to overthink it and reply, *OK.*

After I shower and change, I grab Jennifer's book and my notebook and head downstairs. Jennifer and the pets are in the back yard again.

"I wondered if you were still alive up there." Jennifer tamps the soil down with her hand.

I hold the book out to her. "I'm giving up writing."

She sets her spade down and claps the soil off her gloved hands. She shucks off her gloves and takes the book. "Why?"

"I'll never write anything this good."

She tents her eyes with one hand and looks up at me. "You liked it?"

"I loved it. My only criticism is I would have ended the story with Marie-Laure opening the little house and finding the key."

Jennifer considers this. "But I think the author wanted us to see how Marie-Laure matured." She opens the book. "And you would have missed this line about how the air in a library is a record of every life lived."

I squat next to her and show her the notebook I kept as I read. It's full of words, similes, and sentences from the book. "I haven't had a book affect me this much since

Shadow of the Wind, which, until now, was my favorite book."

She runs her fingers over the cover of Doerr's book. "People often ask me what my favorite book is, but it changes every time I read a great new novel." She scans my list. "I like this observation: 'there are two kinds of mines, both of which will kill you.'" She hands me back Doerr's book. "Keep it. You'll want to read it again, won't you?"

"Yeah. I want to figure out how he broke all the rules of narrative structure and pulled this off."

"Some of the best books break the rules."

I thumb through the pages. "I know this is fiction, but it has history and science in it. Do you think my father would read it?"

"Maybe. But I'll buy him his own copy. You keep this one." She puts her gloves back on and lifts her spade. "By the way, Ash and I enjoyed meeting your friend Peri."

"She likes you guys, too." I don't mention how Peri wants to jump her husband's bones. I stand up. "Well, I'm going to grab something to eat and head out."

"Are you meeting Peri?"

"In a way."

"Have fun."

I like that she doesn't pry, yet I kind of want to tell her that I'm about to bare all for Peri and her friends.

Peri's drawing group meets in one of the classrooms in the art building at UW. I'm fairly familiar with campus since I spent three weeks here earlier this summer. It has begun to drizzle outside so I'm damp when I walk in.

I tap on the open door of the room and a thin blonde woman looks up at me. "Are you Michael?" I nod. "Come on in. I'm Yvonne."

Peri's chatting with a couple of guys when I enter. The tall, skinny one reminds me of Dale. The other guy resembles the actor Zack Galafanakis. Peri waves when she sees me. "You didn't chicken out."

I grin, and stash my hands in my pockets. "I need the money."

Yvonne escorts me to a screen in the corner of the room "Did you bring a robe?" she asks.

"No. Was I supposed to?"

Peri shoots me an apologetic look. "I guess I should have mentioned that."

"Models usually come out wearing one," Yvonne says. "Also, you can cover up during breaks." She thinks for a second. "Follow me." Yvonne leads me to a junk closet overflowing with assorted objects. Images of my mother's living room flash through my head.

Yvonne digs out a sheet that was once white and hands me the cloth. It smells like a dusty old building. "Here. You can use this for now."

We walk back to the classroom; I duck behind the screen and hear a murmur of voices in the room as I shed my clothes.

I drape the sheet around me. Will Peri now picture me naked every time she looks at me? I look down at my thin, but muscular self. This could work to my advantage.

I fling a corner of the dank sheet over my shoulder like a toga and join the artists. Peri stands behind an easel next to a young blonde dude with spiky hair. He and Peri seem to know each other well, and I feel a pull of jealousy. There's also a plump Asian woman, a skinny dude with long hair and a long beard, the chubby guy I noticed earlier, and a pretty woman with long red hair. I'll need to avoid looking at her in order to keep little Mike from standing at attention.

An older guy walks in carrying a large sketch pad, a shoulder bag, and a folded easel. As the gray-haired man sets up, Yvonne plants a wooden chair in the middle of the cluster of easels and places a cushion on it.

Peri grins when she sees me. "You look like a Roman gladiator."

I raise my right arm. "Hail Caesar!"

She laughs, and I know everything will be okay.

Yvonne stands at the center of the room, and says, "Dave can't make it today, so I'll take command." She looks at me. "Peri tells me this is your first-time modeling. Usually for the action poses we have you stand. After that we do a long pose. As a group we'll vote whether to have you sit, lie, or stand. Can you stand in one place for forty-five minutes at a time?"

"I think so."

"Good," she says. "We won't make you pose too precariously. We'll begin with warm up sketches, which progress from fifteen seconds to two minutes. I'll say "switch!" when it's time to change poses."

Yvonne glances at the wall clock. "We'll start doing action sketches in a couple of minutes." She glances at the long-haired guy. "Can we get some music, Steve?"

He flips through a stack of CDs sitting next to a portable CD player and holds one up. "How about we begin with Ravi Shankar?" The group agrees, and he pushes Play.

Immediately I recognize it as something foreign. There's no way this music will give me a boner, so thank you, bearded guy. Still, I won't be able to look directly at the redhead. Or Peri.

Yvonne motions for me to stand in the center of the circle of easels and drawing-donkeys. "Ready?"

"Sure," I say.

"This is Michael, and he's a first-time model, so let's try to make him feel comfortable."

"I'd be way more comfortable if all of you were nude as well," I say.

The chubby guy laughs. "Yeah, that's not going to happen, buddy."

"Just *imagine* we're all naked," Peri adds.

I take a deep breath and drop the sheet. I place my hands on my hips, and immediately hear the scratching of pastel and charcoal against rough paper. As they begin to draw me, I compose a letter in my head to send to Shelly.

Dear Shelly,

I'm naked in front of a group of strangers and one friend. It's not a dream. Or an orgy. If I close my eyes I could be in India as sitars twang and small drums beat in the background. You're thinking to yourself, what the hell is Michael up to now?

I'm modeling for my friend's figure drawing group. And it's oddly relaxing. The warm up poses go quickly, I raise my arms like Atlas, hoping the muscles in my back look sculpted. Yvonne (the lady in charge) yells "switch," and next I hold another pose for two minutes. I crouch, balance on one hand, as if ready to sprint. My knee starts to ache against the tile floor, and I'm relieved to hear "switch!" I stand, arch my back, and study the water stained tile ceiling. The room is cool and my feet are cold against the tile. The Indian drums begin a rapid beat and I feel the urge to run with the music. I hear "switch!" and pose like an archer. By the end of a full two minutes, my biceps burn. For the final warm-up pose, I kneel with my left leg, and my right arm rests on my thigh with my face against my fist, kind of like the Thinker statue. That pose gets murmurs of approval.

"That should be our two-hour pose," one woman says.

I hope she's kidding, because the floor is pressing rudely on my knee, but after a much-needed break, they sit me in a chair for the two-hour long pose, and again I am posed like the Thinker. I'm trying to look contemplative, yet I'm conscious that 1) I should have pissed during the break (it will be half an hour before I get another chance, 2) my elbow is digging into my flesh, and 3) the afternoon sun is blinding me so I have to keep my eyes closed.

With my eyes shut, I'm aware of every sound, the scratch of charcoal against paper as if there are mice inside the walls, a faint aroma of paint, a slap of a brush on canvas, someone rinsing a brush in a water cup and the clatter of a pencil dropping to the floor.

While I keep my eyes closed, films of you run through my head. The day we drove in the country and bought tomatoes and peaches and you fed me slabs of sweet tomato as I steered. Later, we crashed that family picnic. Remember eating Trash Can Dinner? You got to experience how the lower half lives, not like your parents' catered white-table-cloth parties.

Yet you never judged me.

What happened to us, Shelly? We were a unit, lit from within like a five-hundred-watt bulb, entwined like snakes inside a basket. What happened? Oh yeah, Theo happened. And you and the beach boy happened.

Will I always hold that against you? I'm trying not to.

You warned me we'd break up when you chose a college far away. I didn't believe you.

So, you slept with Theo.

Message received. Sometimes I'm a slow learner.

But did you think to ask me what I wanted? Maybe I wasn't ready to move on. Was our relationship just a stepping stone for you? A distraction from the tedium of Rooster, Ohio? Did you use Theo and Maui-beach-bum-dude to carve my heart into a thousand and one pieces?

Did you ever love me?

Did you know, before I learned he was a lying sack of shit, that Theo and I sort of became friends?

I hate to admit that I learned a lot from him, and if it weren't for you, Theo and I might now be buddies. He'd be giving me advice on how to deal with my father, or you. But that ship has sailed.

Yvonne calls for a break and I wrap the sheet around me and dash for the restroom. Now it's the final twenty minutes of the pose.

Maybe it's not such a good idea for me to remain still. I already live inside my head too much. By sitting here, there's nothing to do but think. My butt cheeks are sore, yet a pot full of seventy-five bucks waits at the end of the rainbow.

After I dress, I help Peri pack up her stuff and carry her drawing pads and folding easel to the bus stop. She insists on schlepping the shoulder bag full of drawing supplies, even though it likely weighs more than my load.

"You were great," Peri says. "You're a natural."

"Just call me Nature Boy."

It's raining again, harder than before, and I say, "Wanna stop for coffee? I have money now, so my treat."

We duck into a place called Campus Joe and dump our goods next to a small table. I shell out eighteen bucks of my modeling money for sandwiches, chai lattes, and pastries. But at least we're dry.

"I noticed you worked in charcoal today," I say.

"Until I start drawing, I never know what medium I'll use." She glances out the window. "Maybe it's the rain, but it seemed like a charcoal sort of day."

"May I look?"

She sweeps her hand toward the drawing pad. "Go ahead."

The first couple of pages are filled with line drawings in various media: pencil, pastel and charcoal. The third drawing is the long pose where I'm sitting in the wooden chair. She has drawn me from the neck down and my muscles look awesome.

"I'm not ready to draw your face," she says. "There's something more intimate about portraits than the body."

"Will you hang this in your collection on your bedroom wall?"

"Probably. I want to study how I can improve it."

I close her drawing pad and slide it back in the portfolio. "It looks great to me."

She shrugs. "It's okay. But hey, you survived your first modeling gig."

"I did."

"I always wonder what the models think about when we're staring at them."

"I thought about how the cash would feel in my wallet."

A sadness lingers from my imaginary argument with Shelly. Are she and I better off so many miles apart? If I had gone back to Rooster would I be seeing her everywhere? Yet there's nowhere in Seattle that doesn't remind me of her.

Peri's calm energy is so different from Shelly's. With Shelly I always felt I needed to pay attention to all the details on the map, and with Peri the lines on the map don't have detours.

***

By the time I get home from figure drawing, the sun is out again. Every day the weather wavers between dreary and glorious. I walk the dogs around the neighborhood, listening to *Fall Out Boy* in my ear buds. I try not to think about anything but the music.

The dogs lead me into the house and I hang their leashes on the coat rack near the front door. My father and Jennifer sit in the back yard on the Adirondack chairs, an open bottle of white wine and two glasses on the table between them. Before releasing the hounds into the yard, I observe them. His body language is languid, and as he talks, he gestures and smiles. She responds to something he says, and he laughs heartily.

I hate to break their moment, but the dogs start whining, and Jack scratches at the glass, so I open the French doors. My father turns his head as Jack trots toward them. When he sees me, his brow knits slightly, and the delight he expressed with Jennifer a few seconds earlier dissolves.

Yeah, I'm not imagining things.

I back into the house, close the doors, and head up to my room. My phone has the best cheap therapy: Solitaire. When stuff bugs me or I need to ruminate, I usually run. But modeling and dog walking wore me out. Solitaire is mindless, and it occupies my hands enough so I don't ram my fist through a wall.

I lose the first two games but win the next three. I'm about to begin another round when Peri texts. *-Want to see a free concert?*

Me-Free is my favorite price.

P-Meet me at the Sculpture Park @5:30. Concert starts @6:00.

Sculpture Park. Another place that reminds me of Shelly. Peri picks up on my pause.

P-Is that a problem? Have you had enough of me today?

Me-No, not at all. See you@5:30.

Jennifer and my father are still in the back yard. I poke my head out the door, and say, "I'm meeting Peri for a free concert. See ya later."

"Wait!" Jennifer jumps up and walks toward me. "Are you going to eat dinner there?"

I shrug. "I hadn't thought about it."

"You're like a human garbage disposal. I'll fix you a sandwich so you won't starve."

Jennifer steps inside the house while my father remains outdoors with the dogs and his wine.

"We still have plenty of leftover meatloaf." She places a slab of it between two slices of Dave's Killer Bread. The bread is dark and hearty and may be worth moving to Seattle for. "Which concert are you going to?"

"I'm not sure. Peri said it's a free concert at Sculpture Park."

"Ash and I go to those occasionally." Jennifer wraps my sandwich in waxed paper. She adds a bag of kettle-cooked potato chips and an apple. She reaches into the fridge. "You'll need a bottle of water, too."

"I still can't believe you use disposable water bottles."

"Shhh. Don't tell your father." She stashes all this in a plastic grocery bag. "It's one of the things he's learned to accept about me. I tried using reusable ones, but I keep losing them." She rummages through a cupboard. "Do you want some graham crackers?"

"You know I'll eat pretty much anything."

She smirks, and slides a sleeve of graham crackers in the bag. "It's like raising a goat." She twists the handle shut and hands me the sack.

I grin. "Thanks."

"Do you need to use my car?"

"No. I'll take the bus."

She leans on the counter. "Listen, your father and I are going away for a couple of days."

"Oh?"

"Just a short trip for our fifth anniversary."

"Oh. Happy anniversary."

"Thank you. We'd originally planned to kennel the dogs or have our neighbor check on them, but since you're here, do you mind keeping an eye on them?"

"Not at all."

"We'd invite you along but we only have one room with one bed." She winks at me.

"Oh man, and I was so looking forward to being the third wheel on your romantic getaway." She laughs, and I shove the plastic bag containing my dinner inside my pack. "So where are you going on your getaway?"

"Up to Victoria, British Columbia. "

"When do you leave?"

"Some time tomorrow. We were going to tell you to-night at dinner, but since you won't be here, I'm telling you now."

I hoist my backpack over my shoulder. "Have fun."

"We'll see you in the morning before we leave."

I say goodnight and catch a southbound bus. I've brought a journal and pens just in case something sparks in my brain.

Peri waves when she sees me near the entrance, and the anxiety I felt about coming here disappears. This was the last place Shelly and I explored together in Seattle before everything fell apart. Maybe Peri will reverse the mojo.

She also has a backpack slung over her shoulder. I point out our bags. "You and I look like we're ready to move into a homeless camp."

She shudders. "I don't plan to go back to one anytime soon."

"I don't plan to ever live like that again."

The park is crowded, but we find an open spot where we dump our bags on the ground. Peri removes a blanket from hers, and I help spread it out on the grass.

She pulls various food containers out of her pack: roasted chicken, a wedge of cheese, a bowl of salad, a bag of grapes, a loaf of bread, a thermos filled with coffee, two cups, napkins, plastic forks and knives and a couple more plastic containers.

I set my paltry offerings next to hers. "Sorry, Jennifer only packed for one."

"No problem. This is great. We have a banquet."

We sit cross legged on the blanket facing one another and she passes me a paper plate. "What kind of music is playing tonight?" I ask.

She hands me a chunk of bread. "Jazz."

"Awesome."

She slices off a generous portion of cheese and dumps that on my plate. She adds a bunch of grapes.

I start noshing on my food.

"So, are you okay?" she asks.

"Yeah. Why do you ask?"

"You seemed kind of down after modeling for us."

"Did I?"

"We didn't offend you, did we? Sometimes our conversations get pretty raunchy."

"No, not at all." I pause, recalling bits and pieces of the chatter between the artists as I sank in and out of thoughts about Shelly. "I'm not used to sitting still."

She weighs my words but doesn't take it any further. "Want some coffee? It's decaf."

"Sure."

She reaches for a thermos and I place my hand over hers. "You don't have to serve me, Peri. I won't be able to give you a very good tip."

She snorts. "I'm portioning everything so you don't vacuum up all my food."

"Jennifer says feeding me is like feeding a goat."

"She's not wrong."

"You can have the chicken all to yourself," I say. "I don't eat chicken."

"But you eat other meat?"

"Yeah. It sounds dumb, but I grew to like the chickens on Earl and Dot's farm, so eating it sort of feels like cannibalism."

We dine in companionable silence as we watch people file in. I glance at her, wondering what she's thinking. I give her what I believe is my most seductive grin. "So, are you picturing me naked?"

Her curls bounce as she tilts her head back and laughs. "I picture everyone naked."

"Oh?"

"You did really well today. You didn't seem nervous at all."

"It was unusual at first, but after a while it felt natural to be naked in a room full of clothed people."

She chuckles, and pops a couple of grapes in her mouth.

"What do you do if the model doesn't show up?" I ask.

"Yvonne, Dave, or one of the others will model for us. Yvonne's a great model. She's a yoga teacher so she can bend like Gumby and hold difficult poses for a long time."

"Have you ever posed?"

"I'm not that brave," she says. "I'm working on it, though."

"If you ever *do* model, I think I'll take up figure drawing."

She pops another grape in her mouth. "You'll be waiting a long, long time."

We polish off the cheese and salad, and I stuff a hunk of bread in my mouth.

"Besides baring all for my friends and me today, is anything exciting happening in Michael's world?"

I swallow my bread and gulp some coffee. "Well, I finished an awesome book Jennifer loaned me, I walked the dogs this afternoon, and my father still hates me."

"Don't you think that's your overactive imagination?"

"Jennifer has even noticed. I overheard them discussing it one morning before I went out for a run. I know *you* like him and all, and you're probably picturing *him* naked right now, but…" I shake my head. "He's like reading a book written in a different alphabet."

"You guys just don't know each other."

"I think it's more than that. There's something substantive about me he doesn't like." I bump against her. "Maybe it's because I lack swagger." I pop a few grapes in my mouth. "I'm also disappointed in *him*."

"What *did* you expect?"

"I don't know. But he's not the casual funny guy who appears on his TED talk. At least with me he isn't."

"Maybe if you show interest in his work he might be more accessible. He may even smile at you."

I shudder. "That might be creepy."

She groans at me. "Have you been writing?"

I bite into the meatloaf sandwich. "Not since *The Dirt Thief*." I don't count the deleted and imaginary emails to Shelly.

"Michael, you need to jump back on that writing horse. Don't you have a project due?"

"Yeah, but I don't know *what* my project will be." I look down, pick up the crumbs from my bread and sweep them onto the grass. "I have no idea what or how to connect writing with another discipline."

"Your father's a scientist. Maybe you can extract something from him."

I lie back on the blanket. "That would require having a conversation with him."

She shoves me gently. "Biology tells a story," she says. "Connect the narrative."

I turn my head and look at her. "Do you mean like evolution?"

"Not just evolution, but everyday life. Adaptation and mutation are also stories. Do some reading about what he studies, and then ask him questions as if you're one of his students."

"That's brilliant." I sit up. "That *could* be how I connect with him. Jennifer gave me a copy of his newest book."

"Have you read it?"

"Not yet." I run my hands through my hair.

She reaches over and takes one of my hands. "You need to read his book."

"But what if he's a shitty writer?"

She shoves me. "Get over yourself and read the book."

"You really know how to charm a guy."

She picks up one of the plastic containers. "I have a surprise that will make you feel better about life." She lifts the lid. "I hope you like éclairs."

"What kind of freak doesn't like éclairs?"

She passes the container and a plastic knife to me. I slice the éclair in half, take a piece, and hand her the other half. She lifts her portion, and we bump them together as if toasting wine. I bite into the gushy confection and close my eyes. "Oh man. You really are a bad influence on me."

She giggles. A dot of custard filling rests on the edge of her mouth. I swipe my finger over her lip, lick my finger, and smile. Her dark eyes sparkle back at me with mischief as she savors another bite.

I pop the last bit of pastry in my mouth and Peri hands me a napkin. She pours us each more coffee just as the music starts.

The bass saxophone wails like a lonely city, and the chatter amid the crowd hushes as the drummer steps in and rocks the beat. A guitar sings, and the sax walks in and out. The organist adds his jaunty buzz bop bam. I close my eyes for a few minutes, letting the notes sizzle.

When I open them again, a little boy next to us is dancing to the drum beat. I glance at Peri, smiling, nodding her head to the music.

Jazz always takes me back to my stepfather Bob and good times when I was a kid. Mom was happy then, and our family was whole, and I was that little boy on the blanket next to us, happily dancing as if everyone was watching.

Applause thunders through the crowd at the end of the song and the ground vibrates. I stretch my body out and cross my arms under my head as a pillow.

A soprano sax shrieks, and the trumpet replies in its language of high and low notes. I try to imagine how Kerouac might describe it. *The low hiss of steam and a thunder moon, beep beep beep and the noise of heaven is sweet as whipped cream and skin on skin love on a dark, starry night wise with the lunar language, chittering like crickets on a full moon of long grass, a thunder of stampeding madness and caffeine mysteries.*

If I weren't so comfortable, I'd write that down, but I'm too lazy and mesmerized to get my journal even though my backpack is less than an arm's length away. I tell myself I'll remember my description, knowing I won't, but I don't care. I'm full of jazz and cheese and chocolate éclairs.

I feel the heat of Peri lying next to me. Her eyes are closed, her hands resting on her chest. Her hair splays around her like dark silk, and I'm tempted to kiss those full lips, but don't want to spoil the mood and the music in case she punches me.

At eight o'clock the concert ends, but most of the crowd doesn't jump up and leave. There's still more than an hour of daylight left, and it feels good to lie on the grass amid the mammoth sculptures.

I reach over and wrap a lock of Peri's curly hair in my finger. "That was great. Thanks for asking me." I whip my finger away and her tendril bounces back.

"Music is meant to be shared, and I remembered you like jazz."

"I like you, Persephone Alexandria Diamandis."

She rolls over to face me. "I am pretty great, aren't I?"

I turn and rest my head on my arm and face her. "Do you like me any better now?"

She scrunches her face. "Meh."

"But I posed naked for you. And you brought me an éclair."

"That's only because I didn't want to eat the whole thing myself."

I fiddle with another strand of her corkscrew hair and dangle it in front of my face to make a mustache. "You think I'm charming and debonair and have potential to develop swagger."

Her laughter is music. I carefully place the long piece of hair back on her head and pull her face toward mine. She does not resist, and her lips taste of chocolate and dark coffee.

She pulls back and whispers, "This still doesn't mean I like you."

I give her a Cheshire cat grin. "Yes, you do."

"Even if I *did* like you, I'm not going to date a horny teenage boy," she says.

"But Michael Neruda is twenty-two."

She giggles. I roll her flat onto the ground and pin her hands beneath mine. "Tell me why you like me."

"Someone has to take pity on you. It may as well be me."

I throw my head back and laugh. "But you also find me sexy."

"Only because I've seen you naked."

I give her a lecherous grin. "Maybe it's time to return the favor.

She shoves me off and sits up. "I don't like you *that* well."

I flex my arms for her and she rolls her eyes. But then she kisses me lightly on the lips. "We should probably clear out of here before dark."

Peri and I clean up our picnic and walk to the bus stop. "I'm going to see you home," I say. "It will be dark by the time you make it to Ravenna."

"You're a scholar and a gentleman."

"I wouldn't call me a scholar. Just a guy who carries around a dictionary and a thesaurus."

Peri and I hold hands on the bus. At her stop, we amble toward her house. I wonder if her parents are watching through a window. Her mother is pretty protective, but Mr. Diamandis doesn't reek of the let-me-get-my-gun vibe. Still, I pull Peri to a darkened section of the front stoop and kiss her again.

"Thanks again for inviting me out tonight," I say. "It was a peanut butter and honey evening with orange music and a butterfly kiss on the soul."

She cocks her head and eyes me. "You always have the most unusual way of putting things."

"You're like hot buttered toast on a Saturday morning. You're warm and soft like a blanket fresh from the dryer."

She touches my face. "Maybe now I like you a teeny bit more."

"Does that mean I'll see you tomorrow?"

She grins. "Probably. I'd invite you in, but I'm working the early shift tomorrow." She grabs the knob to her front door and turns it. "Read your father's book."

I wave, watch her step inside, and make my way to the bus stop.

Once at home, I yank my father's book off the shelf and study the author photo, his Hollywood handsome smile, the smile he reserves for everybody but me. "Please don't be shitty," I tell the book. I crack it open and the aroma of new book drifts up. That smell is like walking outside on a hot day and being handed a glass of ice-cold lemonade. I begin to read.

I do not know what I appear to the world, but to myself I seem to have been only like a boy playing on the sea shore, and diverting myself in now and then finding a smoother pebble or a prettier shell than ordinary, whilst the great ocean of truth lay all undiscovered before me.
Isaac Newton

My earliest memory is looking out the window and studying rain. Even at three years-old, I knew water was special, and I wondered from where water and rain origi-nated. Everything else around me was solid and tangible, yet here was this clear substance falling from the sky, fill-ing the tub for my bath and boiling on the stove for my mother's tea.

In school I learned water could be broken down to a formula of two hydrogen atoms and one oxygen atom. But I also knew our most abundant resource was more than a few letters and numbers.

More than 70% of earth is water. It has a long, complex history on our planet. Water is central to all life in the uni-verse.

This early obsession with water led me to become an ocean biologist. The thrust of my practice and research is sea life, particularly sea turtles, but we cannot marginalize and isolate one life from another. The sea sustains us, and as a scientist and a human being, I study the ocean in all its aspects. This is particularly important now because, pardon my pun, the oceans are drowning in pollution.

In Spanish the word pacifico means peaceful, yet one need only spend time at sea to know the Pacific, or any other ocean, is anything but peaceful. While change is constant, our seas have suffered unnatural, accelerated damage in the past twenty-five years. Our oceans now act as dumping grounds for human waste and castoffs.

My goals with this book are to provide a brief understanding on the chemistry of water, to demonstrate how our planet is in constant flux, to introduce the reader to the universe under the oceans' surfaces, to illustrate how man has disturbed and exacerbated the oceans' natural evolution through personal and industrial pollution, and finally, to show how this shift in global balance has caused deadly temperature changes.

The scope of this book is for the lay scientist and the enquiring yet uninformed consumer, because it's not just scientists who will determine the future of our planet. Each one of us has a stake in preserving our world. At this writing, the ocean has already been depleted of nearly 80% of its coral reefs and megafauna, which include sharks, dolphins, large fishes, and turtles, with an alarming increase in the numbers of species at risk for extinction in the next decade...

Relieved that my father's book doesn't stink so far, I stay up late, and end up reading half of it.

In my waking dream I am swimming next to an eel. It gazes at me with its beady eye, snaps its jaw open and closed a few times and swims away.

Chapter Thirteen

Jennifer sits out back drinking her morning coffee. She turns when she hears my footsteps. "How was your concert last night?"

"Fantastic." I plunk down in the adjacent chair and set my cup on the table. "I had to throw away your plastic bag, though. I hope the trash Nazis don't track you down and arrest you."

"Will you smuggle books to me if they put me in Garbage jail?"

"Sure." I glance around. "Where's...?"

"Your father?" she says.

I give her a sheepish grin and gulp some coffee. "I don't know what to call him. He's not my dad. And he's not old enough to be referred to as Pops. But I don't feel comfortable calling him Ash like you do." I shrug. "My friend Shoe says I should call him Doc."

"Ask him what he wants you to call him."

"That's the thing. I feel awkward asking him direct questions."

"Why?"

"I think you've noticed he and I don't connect."

She grabs for her cup and sputters a noise of exasperation. "You're like two rams butting horns."

"Peri gave me an idea on how to break the ice." I set my father's book on the table.

"You're reading Ash's book! What do you think of it?"

"It's good so far. Scary, too."

"I won't spoil the end by revealing the butler did it," she says. "So, what's your idea?"

"Well, I have this portfolio assignment due in order to get credit for the writing workshop. We're supposed to take another discipline and tie it to the writing process. Last night Peri reminded me that biology tells a story, and she suggested I interview him about some of what's in his book."

"That's a great idea." She sips and nods. "Finish his book while we're gone, and when we get back, you'll have a better idea on how to begin a dialogue with him."

"When are you leaving?"

"As soon as Ash finishes packing the Subaru."

"Hey, would it be okay if Peri came over while you guys are out of town?"

"Sure. Just don't have any wild parties."

"Ha! I only know one person in Seattle." Two, if you count Dale. Well, three, but I don't count Theo.

The thump of dog feet is followed by the clink of collars. I turn, and my father follows behind Jack and Lucy. "The car's all loaded up, Jen. I put the wetsuits in the..." He stops when he notices me. "Oh. Good morning. I didn't realize you were up."

Jennifer reaches out and touches my arm. "I made a list of emergency contact numbers if you can't find either of us. It's on the kitchen counter."

"We might be underwater," he says. "We're taking a couple of dives."

"Or under the sheets," Jennifer adds with a wink. My face flushes.

She gets up and grabs her coffee cup. "By the way, I loved *Kafka on the Shore*. I'll go get that for you." She gently bumps the top of my head with her fist. "Tell Ash your idea."

I hold up his book. "I've been reading this, and I wondered if I could interview you for my portfolio project. When you get back from Canada, of course."

"Are you interested in marine science?" He claims Jennifer's empty seat. Jack and Lucy sniff around the yard.

"I wasn't until I started reading your book."

"Glad to know I may have a convert."

"So, while you're gone, I was thinking I'd finish this and come up with some questions if that's okay," I say.

"That would be fine."

Jennifer returns and hands me the Murakami book. "I loved it. It's eccentric, but you're an odd duck, too."

I chuckle. "Thanks. I'll start it this weekend." I nod toward my father. "After I finish *his* book."

My father stands. "We'll be back Sunday night. Please don't burn down our house."

"I'm leaving my car keys for you as well," Jennifer says. "They're on the key rack in the kitchen."

My father tussles with Jack for a minute. He picks up Lucy, nuzzles her, and sets her back on the ground. "You two be good," he says to the dogs, and walks toward the house.

Jennifer raises a finger to both animals as if teaching them a class. "No parties, okay?" She grabs Jack's snout. "Keep an eye on your big brother Michael. He's new around here, so make sure he doesn't get lost."

She gives me a quick hug before joining my father at the door. He waves, slides an arm around Jennifer's waist, and they vanish into the garage.

As soon as they back out of the driveway, I pick up the two books and go inside, where I notice the list of phone numbers Jennifer left on the kitchen counter. Jennifer also left three twenty-dollar bills under her note. The attached Post-it says: *Pizza money, so you don't starve. There's also lasagna in the freezer and salad and fruit in the fridge. Have fun.*

I refill my coffee cup and text Peri. -*Have the house to myself all weekend. Want to come over and keep a lonely guy company?*

P-*Does that mean hot dad won't be there?*

Me-*Sorry. He went swashbuckling with Jennifer.*

P-*Darn. Guess I'll still come. Working until 3 or so.*

Me-*I'll handle dinner. Lasagna!*

I wander to the living room. The energy inside is changed, as if the house sags in my father's and Jennifer's absences. Clocks that never ticked before announce their presence and new creaks crackle through the wooden floorboards.

I stroll into my father's study. Bookshelves cover three of the walls. His desk sits between two bookcases in front of the window. I open the blinds, and am rewarded with a spectacular view of the lake. Sun casts shadows throughout the room, illuminating a giant framed poster of a scary looking fish. The caption reads, "When you're down by the sea and an eel bites your knee, that's a moray."

Framed photos of him with a dive team on a boat and a couple of pictures of sea turtles hang on the same wall.

On his desk rests a framed picture of him and Jennifer together on a beach. Jennifer wears nothing but a hot pink bikini and a bridal veil, my father sports flowered swim trunks. Both of them smile broadly and hold up flutes of champagne.

One bookshelf contains old record albums and a giant stereo system. My father seems like one of those guys who are picky about their vinyl. He probably has his stereo booby-trapped with a microscopic hair that triggers an alarm.

Yet I'm curious about his musical taste. The albums and CDs are arranged by genre. His 90's high school rock CDs butt up against old jazz, blues and classic rock albums. My father's a white version of Bob! I carefully slide out one of the vinyl records from his collection and mark the spot with a ruler from his desk.

The album in my hands is Tom Waits' Used Songs 1973-1980. On the black and white cover, Waits leans against an old Pontiac. One of the songs on this record, *Blue Valentines,* reminds me of Shelly and the day she and I sat by her pool, trying to sing along like Waits. We had all the dogs in her neighborhood howling.

Thinking about Shelly right now doesn't feel like a knife twisting in my chest. Am I finally over her?

I flick the power button on the stereo system, lift the cover on the record player, and carefully glide the vinyl out of its liner. Bob taught me to "always hold them by the edges." He'd demonstrate by holding a record against his palms rather than grasping it with his fingers.

I place the 33 on the spindle and gently set the needle on the grooves. The sound, even though it pops a couple of times, comes out full and round. I crank the volume. My father has an awesome speaker system.

As the music plays in the background, my fingers travel along the spines of his books. Some people, like Shelly's mother, shelve books by color. I figure my father might arrange his books by topic like his albums, but an Archeology text leans against a book of quotations. Adjacent to that is Shakespeare's Collected Works. A thick book called History of Art stands next to an oceanography textbook. I wonder if this haphazard arrangement drives his librarian wife nuts.

His high school yearbooks are on a lower shelf and I pull off the one from his and my mother's senior year. The inside cover and pages are covered in autographs. Ellie, his awful girlfriend, took up an entire page with her loopy handwriting and drawings of hearts and flowers and lip prints. She wrote some sickening crap about how he was 'the awesomest guy ever' and she hoped they would 'be together until time stops.' Jeez. What was he thinking by dating her? Lucky for him he evolved enough to find Jennifer.

Near the back, my mother wrote, "thanks for the tutoring sessions. You're my favorite teacher." She added a line drawing of a cat and signed it 'Susan F.' No mention of their hot sessions in the prop room under the stage.

I flip to my father's formal senior picture, the one that confirmed for Shelly and me that Ashton Meadows is my father. With my phone I snap photos of my father and mother's yearbook pictures. I place them in split screen and look at my heritage. They look good together.

Near the yearbooks are two photo albums. I slide these out and rest them on the desk top. The first one contains old family photos. The petite red-headed woman surrounded by three small kids must be his mother. My grandmother. The boy and girl next to my father are my aunt and uncle. Unlike Jeff, Annie, and me, there's a familial resemblance between my father and his siblings. These strangers are also my family.

A few pages later, a formal family portrait fills the page. My father's father stands in the back. He's a good-looking guy wearing a suit. In this photo my grandmother's shoulder-length hair is blonde.

I flip through the album to see if there are more recent photos. My aunt's wedding. My father and his brother stand looking uncomfortable in suits. Their mother's hair is short and dark. I wonder what color it is now.

Toward the back of the book are a few pictures of my uncle with his wife and daughter. He looks like a heavier version of my father. Jennifer told me my uncle teaches high school math.

The other photo album contains pictures of my father on various expeditions. His appearance has changed little over the years.

Side one of the record finishes. I lift the needle, shut down the stereo, and place the vinyl back in its slot. I also slide the photo albums back on the bookshelf. Like a detective, I inspect the office to see if anything looks amiss. I close the blinds and trek upstairs.

The door to Jennifer and my father's bedroom stands ajar. Lucy sleeps at the foot of their massive bed. I push the door all the way open, where it is both light and dark. The walls are painted a deep green, but two large windows facing the lake give the room a glow. A faint smell of Polo men's cologne hangs in the air. I became sort of an expert on men's fragrances when I lived in my car. I used to swipe the sample pages out of men's magazines at the library and wipe them on my skin. I was the best smelling vagrant you'd ever meet.

On top of one nightstand rests a book called *Orcas and Man: What Killer Whales Can Teach Us*. Ocean nerd. No doubt his side of the bed. The book lies on top of several issues of *The New Yorker* and *The Atlantic*. I slide open the drawer. Inside are a flashlight, two pairs of glasses, several pens, Burt's Bees lip balm, a pack of mints, a package of lined note cards, a storm weather radio, nail clippers, alcohol swabs, a box of 'ribbed for her pleasure' condoms, dental floss, and a bottle of Aleve. If I were writing a story about this guy it would begin, *He was a man prepared for romance and disaster*.

I creep over to Jennifer's side. Her nightstand is piled with six books, all fiction, and a stack of women's magazines. I'm tempted to open her drawer, too, but stop myself. What if she really *does* keep whips and chains in there? I don't want that picture in my head. I often hear laughter and murmured conversation before the sound of lovemaking filters upstairs. Yeah, some drawers are better left unopened.

Lucy stirs, blinks her eyes and whines. I stroke her head and walk to the mirrored dresser where I spot the bottle of Polo. I spray my T-shirt with it, and memories of Shelly flood my brain. I recap the bottle and set it down. She liked when I wore this.

The dog yawns and jumps off the bed. She wags her little tail and looks up at me.

"Are you going to tell your mommy I poked around her bedroom?" I pick Lucy up and carry her downstairs to the kitchen.

I grab a banana, and both dogs follow me to the back yard. I slump into one of the Adirondack chairs and stare at the photos I snapped of my biological parents. In these head shots you can't tell which one is rich and which one is poor. They're both slightly sad, good-looking kids.

I close my photo app and open my father's book. As I read, I compose questions in a notebook.

His chapter on pollution and how sea animals get caught by or feed on plastic bags makes me feel guilty for tossing out Jennifer's grocery bag. I also regret every plastic bottle I've ever discarded.

The book includes a chapter on his research in the Hawaiian Islands. While there, he and the dive team found dozens of turtles, whales, sharks, dolphins, and other sea life strangled by plastic debris polluting the beaches. He notes this is common no matter where he dives, be it Costa Rica, Canada, or the United States, yet Hawaiian beaches are among the dirtiest.

In the book's conclusion, he states, "We've become a world of blind polluters, as if the earth is a garbage bin and not the thing that sustains us. Planet earth is a living, breathing entity. Perhaps the term Mother Earth needs to be used more frequently. Would you treat your mother the way we treat oceans and land forms? Your mother may have helped you clean your room, but she cannot clear up the masses of trash you leave behind each day."

Ha! *My* mother couldn't begin to straighten up *her* mounds of beloved garbage. I learned how *not* to clean by living with her.

My phone buzzes. I glance at the time. 3:15.

Peri texts-*Off now. What time should I come over?"*

Me-Any time.

P-Maybe 5?

Me-Sounds good.

If it weren't so warm out, I'd go for a run, but the temperature is now eighty-six, so I remain in the backyard under a tree and re-read sections of my father's book.

Sleepy from the heat, I close my eyes and drift off. I'm surrounded by blue, a perfect aqua blue like a gemstone, and the blue floats toward me, swaying through the water like a long-tailed fish. I bite down on the colorful treat and try to swallow. The blue gets stuck in my throat and I gasp for breath. Alarm bells sound. Insistent buzzing.

I wake and grab my phone. "Hello!"

"Are you running?"

"No, I was asleep. I dreamed I was suffocating on a plastic bag."

"Ew! It's a good thing I woke you up."

133

Jack jumps up to greet Peri, and Lucy barks a hello. Peri pets the dogs with one hand and holds up a pastry box with the other.

"It's your fault I swallowed a plastic bag," I say.

She steps inside. "How is it my fault?"

I lead her into the kitchen and turn on both ceiling fans. "You made me read the Dr. Oz of Oceanography's book."

"Is it any good?" She perches on one of the barstools and places the box on the counter.

I sit at the next stool. "It's great. Scary, though."

"Scary how?"

"Basically, the environment is screwed." I press my thumb and forefinger together. "We're this close to the point of no return."

She scrunches her face. "Does he say how we can we fix it?"

"He offers a few suggestions." I stand up and offer her something to drink.

"A glass of water."

I fill two glasses with ice and pour from the Brita pitcher. I peek inside the box. "It looks like a cake of some sort."

"It's tiramisu."

"Sounds Greek to me."

"Actually, it's Italian." She rests her elbows on the counter. "You said you were fixing lasagna for dinner, so I thought I'd stick to the theme."

"Or I can order pizza."

She tilts her glass to her lips and shrugs. "Either's fine with me. I'm not all that hungry yet."

"Me neither." I pull my T-shirt away from my skin even though the ceiling fans are running full blast. "It's still stuffy in here. Do you want to sit outside? It's slightly less hot out there."

"Okay." She puts the pastry box in the fridge and picks up our water glasses. I grab a bag of corn chips, and the dogs accompany us outdoors. We tilt the umbrella over the table to create more shade.

Peri shucks off her sandals and buries her toes in the grass. "Ahhh. That feels better. We were uber busy today. My feet are killing me."

She lifts my father's book and skims the front and back covers. "I might want to borrow this when you're finished."

"You just want to ogle at the swashbuckler's picture."

She laughs, and sets the book back on the table. "Guilty as charged." She sips her water and glances at the Murakami book.

"Jennifer loaned me that one. Her book club is reading it." Peri nods and reads the inside flap. "She says it's kind of weird, which is why she thinks I'd like it."

Peri places *Kafka On the Shore* on top of my father's book. "I liked his book *Norwegian Wood*. It was odd, too, but in a good way."

"The character named Midori reminds me of Shelly," I say.

"Hmmm." Peri arranges her bare feet in my lap. "You still miss her, don't you?"

I massage the soles of her feet. "It's odd to wake up every day and remember I won't see her."

Peri lolls her head back, closes her eyes, and sighs. "You're good at that."

"I used to do this for my mom. She works as a nurse's aide."

Peri looks up. "You miss your family, too, don't you?"

I press down with my knuckles on the fleshy part right behind Peri's toes. She flinches, but my mom always told me it hurt in a good way. "Yeah. Especially my sister. She's got a good thing going with Dot and Earl, but I still worry because she's kind of written Mom off. Annie hasn't seen our Mom since she moved out a year ago."

"That's so sad. My mother gets on my nerves, but I can't imagine not talking to her every day."

Peri tilts her head back again and her curls glow red in the sunlight. "You look like an apparition with the sun behind you," I say. "You have a red halo."

"Maybe I *am* an apparition and you're still dreaming."

"At least you're not an eel." My thumbs bear down on the bottom of her heel. Peri jerks back, but she doesn't pull her foot away. I knead more gently, working my fingers up to her ankles and calves. Peri doesn't resist when my hands glide over her thighs. "Body of a woman, white hills, white thighs…"

She opens her eyes and gazes at me. "Are you quoting poetry or writing one of our own?"

"I'm quoting Neruda."

"You've memorized a lot of poetry."

"Mainly Neruda."

"That's why Shelly calls you Michael Neruda."

"Yes."

"Does it bother you to talk about her?"

My fingers trickle along her skin down to her knees.

"Not at the moment." I rub at a spot just below her knee. "Your tibialis is swollen."

She gazes at me. "You know some anatomy."

I nod. "Coach made us learn the names of muscles and bones for Cross Country. In case we were injured, we could pinpoint exactly where."

"In school I learned artists' anatomy to know the shape of bones and muscles under the skin."

I knuckle walk her calf muscles. "Mmmmmm," she says. "You should get a job as a massage therapist. I'm in heaven."

My fingers skate up to her thighs again. "Your skin is the silk of a rose petal."

"Neruda again?"

"Nope. Michael G. Flynn."

"What's the G stand for?"

"Gillam. My late uncle was named Gillam."

"That's an unusual name."

I squeeze her calves as if kneading bread dough. "My grandmother was into some 70's rock band named Gillam, so she named my uncle after them."

"It's a shame you never got to meet him."

"It is." I graze my knuckles over her soleus and fibula. "From what I know he was cool. My brother's dad and he were BFFs."

Jack snorts in his sleep as Jack's Cat crawls over and curls his body next to the dog. I love their cross-species friendship. They make love stories look easy.

137

"How old were you the first time?" I ask.

"The first time I had sex?"

I nod.

"Seventeen. How about you?"

"Seventeen."

"That must be the magic number."

"If you believe all the locker room talk, I was pretty much the last virgin in boys cross country."

"Did the guys tease you about it?"

"No. I didn't kiss and tell. It's not fair to the other person to reveal details about ...you know."

She grins. "Girls talk about 'you know' too. Some of my high school friends started having sex as freshmen."

"At that age my friend Rick and I were still gawking at pictures of naked ladies in *National Geographic*. When we were library aides, we'd sneak into the magazine storage room and look at old issues. We marked pages with the best boobs with post-it notes."

"And the librarian never caught on?"

"I don't think she ever went back there," I say. "Mrs. Morgan usually sent aides to fetch stuff out of the store room."

"Do they still publish that?"

"I think so." Peri doesn't resist when my fingers trail up her thighs to the bottom of her shorts.

"Did you enjoy it?" She asks.

"Sex, or looking at *National Geographic*?"

"Ha ha."

"Sex was better than I imagined," I say.

"In what ways?"

"There's nothing quite like the soft heat of flesh against flesh. It's like having bolts of lightning strike, and if they kill you, you don't mind because your whole body is electric."

My fingers sink deep into her thigh muscles. "How about you? Was your first time good?"

"It was…. awkward," she says. "I don't like for just anyone to touch me. There has to be a shared energy, otherwise it's gross."

My palms rest on her knees. "So, my touching you doesn't gross you out?"

"If it did, you'd have gotten a knee in the nuts."

I chuckle.

She leans toward me and our lips meet. She slides onto my lap and live wires quiver around us. "So, the swashbuckler and Jennifer left you alone the whole weekend?"

"The whole weekend."

"Do you want to take this upstairs?" she asks.

"Um, yeah."

We take our water glasses and step over the animals as they sleep in the sun and enter the French doors. Peri stops halfway up the staircase to study the painting on the wall.

"Jennifer told me she painted it in college. It's kind of a cool landscape, isn't it?"

Peri gasps. "Michael, it's not a landscape. It's a nude."

"It is?" I eye the picture more closely.

"Yes." Peri points to what I believed were hills. "These are breasts." Her hand sweeps to the foreground. "And this is the model's torso."

"Huh. What do you know?"

"Have you ever even *seen* breasts?" Peri asks.

I give her a sheepish grin and feign a hillbilly accent. "No ma'am. Girls in Rooster don't gots 'em."

She grabs my hand and climbs the stairs ahead of me. "Come on, you."

At the top of the stairs, Peri peers inside the open door of my father's bedroom. "Is this where the swashbuckler sleeps?"

I push her away from the door. "We're not doing it in his bed." She makes a frownie face. "Wait here." I stalk into the bedroom and steal a couple of condoms from my father's nightstand. Then I lead Peri up one more flight.

Inside my room, I open the music app on my phone. "What should we listen to?"

"Something romantic. Adele?"

"I thought Adele made girls cry."

"It makes great sex music. It's sad and emotional."

"I don't have any Adele."

She takes her phone out of her back pocket and Adele fills the room with her husky voice.

Peri and I face each other on my bed. "Just remember," she says. "We're friends, but now there are benefits."

I reach out and caress her face. "Does that make you my benefactor?"

"I've already seen you naked, so at least there aren't any unpleasant surprises ahead."

I snort a laugh and pull her toward me for a kiss. "Now it's my turn to see *you* naked." Our lips devour one another. Adele wails, and the bass notes announce our point of no return.

She pulls back and whispers. "Take off your shirt."

One-handed, I wrench my T-shirt off and fling it across the room. Her warm hands rest on my skin and her fingers read my flesh. I'm sinking and soaring.

Peri nudges me back onto the mattress. She draws a slow, invisible line from my forehead down to my belly button. Electric currents surge through my body. She stops, unbuttons her blouse, and tosses it to the floor. Her large breasts beckon across the top of a pink lacy bra. I reach out to touch them, but she waggles a finger at me. "Not yet."

She closes her eyes and runs her palm flat across my belly as if smoothing sand on the beach. Adele wails, "I can't looove youu in the daaaark..." Peri's breasts shimmy under the lace, her long hair tickles my skin. My flesh is a live circuit.

Peri unhooks the button on my shorts and tugs on the zipper one tooth at a time. It's both excruciating and exquisite. She grips the legs of my shorts and I help her slide them off. Violins float into a crescendo and I am wearing only boxers.

She stands up, reaches behind her, and unhooks her bra. That, too, lands on the floor. The sun through the window-blinds paints stripes over her full, silky body.

"This is what breasts look like." She steps out of her shorts and panties. "And this is what a nude looks like."

I give a short laugh and reach for her. "I like this landscape."

She lies down next to me and takes my hand. "Close your eyes."

"But I'm enjoying the view."

"Trust me on this." I shut my eyes. "Describe what you feel as you touch me. Make my body into a poem."

Two velvet moons,
the scent of coconut and earth,
your breasts are the landscape of my desire.

Skin as delicate as the inside of a flower,
Satiny, and stained with my fingertips,
Your breasts are fire to my coal.

Your waist is a tapered candle,
Your thighs are silken anchors,
Your hips are my salvation.

Chapter Fourteen

Peri and I lie side by side in the darkened room, the ceiling fan whirring above us, her sleeping body all hills and valleys. I glide my hand over her and she murmurs and opens her eyes.

"Hi."

"Hmmmmm." Her voice is full of sleep. She rolls onto her back and her eyes flash open. "What time is it?"

I check my phone. "Ten-fifteen."

"Oh crap." Peri sits up. "I have to work the early shift tomorrow." She gets out of bed and gathers her clothes. I slip into my boxers and she tosses me my T-shirt.

"You could spend the night."

"You've met my mother," she says. "Do you really think that would happen?"

"Yeah. I guess not."

She clasps her bra behind her. "This was fun, though."

"It was." I zip up my shorts. "But we never ate dinner."

She shrugs. "It's kind of too hot to eat."

As we walk into the kitchen, Jack stirs by the back door. "Are you hungry?" He harrumphs. "Come on, buddy." I fill the dogs' food and water bowls.

Peri stands at the sink sipping tap water. "What are you thinking about?"

I close the dog food container. "That this is awkward and I'm a little hungry."

"We could always eat a piece of tiramisu."

"Sounds good to me."

She opens the fridge and pulls out the pastry box. "This is best with coffee or espresso, but it's too late for caffeine."

"How about with a glass of wine?"

"That would work."

I open my father's wine cooler. "What kind?"

She glances through the labels and pulls out a bottle of white." Orvieto is a nice, light wine." Like Shelly, Peri seems to know about wine.

I've watched Jennifer and my father operate the wine opening gizmo several times, but my attempt is an epic fail. I get the opener stuck in the cork.

"You went too deep," Peri touches a button. The opener retracts, but is still jammed. "Do you have a regular corkscrew?"

"I dunno." We look through several drawers until Peri finds one.

She winds the thing inside the bottle and pops the cork. "There's still pieces of cork inside, but we can pick them out." Peri pours us each a glass.

I find a jazz station on the radio. "Should we eat the cake right out the box or be civilized and cut it?"

"Let's be civilized," she says.

I gather two small plates, two forks and a large knife. "How do we cut this?"

Peri takes the knife and slices us each a slab of dessert. We carry our plates and glasses outside.

There's a lighter on the table and I flick it on to light the tiki torches.

"This is nice," Peri sits in one of the Adirondack chairs. "It feels cooler now." She picks up her glass and the wine shimmers in the torch glow. Her skin is amber. If I reach out to touch her I know she will feel like velvet.

"So." I take a slug of wine and set my glass down. "This day turned out well."

"It did." She dips her fork into the cake. "And you finally got to see me naked."

"About damn time." The darkness hides my flushed grin. The pianist dashes his fingers over the piano keys while a bass player and drummer keep pace. I tap my foot along to the music, the taste of wine and coffee custard on my tongue. Above us, under a nearly moonless light, I can make out several faint stars. "The word of the day is stelliferous. "

"What does it mean?"

"Look up."

"Does it have to do with stars?"

"It does."

She smirks. "Isn't gazing at stars kind of a romantic cliché?"

"It totally is." The song on the radio is *Take Five* by The Dave Brubeck Quartet. The music takes me back to a candlelit evening when I was a kid. Mom and Bob filled our house with jazz, and the two of them snuggled on the couch, often holding my baby sister Annie. Jeff and I created Lego cities on the floor, and the jazz notes influenced my color choices. Sonny Rollins made me choose red Legos. Miles Davis prompted me to build blue and green cities. I created a whole series of yellow floors on a building when Bob played his vinyl *Take Five* album.

When the song ends, the announcer on the radio says, "You've been listening to The Dave Brubeck Quartet with selections from the 1958 Newport Jazz Festival live album."

"You chose good music," she says.

I hold out my wine glass like a salute. "Thanks."

She takes another bite of cake and settles into the seat. The announcer says, "Next we'll be listening to a selection from Big Maybelle called *Candy*."

The song starts, and I stand and reach for her hand. "And here's another romantic cliché: dancing by torch light."

She grins, takes my hand, and I lead her across the brick patio.

We sway against one another, the notes revealing their shades of yellow, orange and purple. Under a stelliferous sky with a girl in my arms, the evening is too bright for me to feel blue.

Chapter Fifteen

Around midnight I drive Peri back home in Jennifer's car. "Will I see you tomorrow, or have you had enough of me?"

She unfastens her seatbelt. "I'm working."

"I could come by the bookstore."

"Sure."

I unlatch my seatbelt. "I'll walk you to the door."

We walk hand in hand to her front step. Her enormous cat scowls up at me as if I've just asked him to loan us twenty bucks. Peri picks up the furry beast and cradles him. "Pooh, you remember Michael."

The cat is not impressed and buries his head against Peri's chest. She strokes his fur. "I've had Pooh since he was a kitten, so he thinks I'm his mother."

"It's hard to kiss a girl goodnight with a barrier of fur between you."

She holds her face up and I kiss her until the cat meows for us to break it up. "I enjoyed today."

"Me, too."

When I get back to my father's, I eat a second piece of tiramisu and place our glasses and plates in the dishwasher. I turn out the lights, and make sure the doors are locked. The dogs accompany me upstairs.

Jack's Cat is already asleep in the messy center of my bedding. I strip down to my boxers and find a spot on the bed. With my father and Jennifer gone, all three of the animals sleep with me, making the warm night even warmer, but I drift off to sleep almost immediately.

Jack's Cat walks on my head around seven-thirty to remind me it's time to feed the cat. I lumber down the steps, unlock the back door to let the dogs out, and open a can of Fancy Feast. Jack's Cat will only eat smelly fish flavors.

After a mug of coffee, I'm finally awake. I consider texting Peri but she's already at work. I eat breakfast, dress, and take the dogs for a walk around the neighborhood. Then I load my backpack and head to Emerald City Books.

The coffee shop buzzes with activity. After I buy a muffin and a large coffee, I manage to score a small table to myself. From my seat, I watch Peri tend to her customers and am envious of how they occupy her attention. Do I have the right to feel possessive about my friend with the awesome benefits?

I plug in my ear buds and open my journal. The blank, lined page stares back at me. It's been a couple weeks since I've written anything except emails, but today feels different, as if the weight of words has been lifted and I can once again form sentences.

Peri sits across from me and I look up. "Hey, you're writing again."

"It's garbage, but at least the pen is moving."

She beams at me. "I guess you just needed to get laid to cure your writer's block."

I toss my head back and laugh. "You should advertise your services in Writer's Digest. You could make a fortune."

"My mother would love that," she says. "She's still freaked out that I draw naked men." Peri glances at the paragraphs I've written. "What's your story about?"

"It's not a story yet. Just a bunch of wordplay nonsense."

"Maybe you need more motivation sessions."

I close my notebook. "I think you may be right."

***

Peri and I spend the rest of the weekend exploring Seattle. Like Shelly, she likes riding in the car with the windows open on the freeway, her hair billowing around her like a mermaid underwater. On Sunday we cruise up to Bellingham and eat lunch at The Village Bookstore. Her parents expect her back for Sunday dinner, so we come back to Seattle around 4:30. Mrs. Diamandis invites me to join them, but I decline. Peri seems relieved.

Back at the house, I throw a load of laundry in the washer and the dogs and I sit out back and read from *Kafka on the Shore*. Jack sniffs around in Jennifer's garden patch until we hear the garage door open.

Jack's Cat leaps off my lap and Jack and Lucy dash toward the house. I rub at the claw marks on my thighs and saunter in after the pets.

Jennifer bends down and the dogs shower her with affection. "Did you two behave?" They bark replies in dog language. "Who's a good dog? Who's been a good dog?"

She eyes me up and down. "You look rested. You must have had a good weekend." She winks, and sets her purse on the counter.

"I did. How was yours?"

"It was fabulous." She pulls a bottle of white wine from the wine cooler and inserts the wine gizmo to uncork it. Evidently, I didn't break it. "Traffic was a pain in the ass, so we need wine."

My father carries two canvas duffels in from the garage. He sets the bags down and stoops to let the dogs jump up and greet him.

Jennifer hands him a glass of wine. He smiles and takes a nip. "Ahhhh. That hits the spot."

"Your father's vocabulary is quite colorful when he's behind the wheel." Jennifer takes a swig and sets her glass on the counter. "So, what did you do over the weekend?"

I gesture to my father. "I finished his book."

"Oh?" He seems surprised.

"I'm ready to interview you any time."

He glances at his glass. "I was just headed out back to recover from the drive."

I place my book on the counter. "There's no hurry."

My father tops off his glass. "Just give me a few minutes to decompress and come out back."

"Okay. I'll go get my notes."

He nods. "See you outside." Jack and Lucy skitter after him.

Upstairs, I root through the stuff on my desk. After I collect a notebook, his book, and a book on ocean life I borrowed from his study, I meet my father in the back yard.

Jack rests at my father's feet and there are two glasses of wine on the table. I sit adjacent to him at the cafe table. "Is Jennifer joining us?"

"No. Jen wants to unpack and do laundry." He indicates the extra glass. "That's for you."

"Thanks." I take a gulp.

He eyes me. "What's your first question?"

I reach for my pen and open the notebook. "Why turtles? What is it about them that attracted you?"

He fingers the stem of his glass. "It was sort of by accident, and it concerned a girl."

I form a half smile. "All my life's accidents concern girls."

He chuffs a laugh. "Yeah, but we can't live without them."

My father and I tip our glasses, and he gives me a thoughtful look. "When I was an undergrad at Ohio State, I heard about a summer internship between my junior and senior year. Part of the attraction was it took place in Costa Rica, so I thought this would be a good place to practice my Spanish. But the *main* attraction was a biology major named Heidi who had also signed up. I figured this was a prime opportunity to get her alone on a beach and let nature take its course."

"How did that work out?"

He drinks some wine and sets his glass on the table. "It turns out *she* had eyes for a grad student who was also part of the crew." He sighs and gazes at the back fence.

"I was kept busy, though. One of my tasks was tagging sea turtles, and I developed a real passion for them."

"How was your Spanish?"

"*Las Tortugas son consideradas simbolos largas vidas y las tenacidad seperate de muchas culuras.*"

"I guess that answers *that* question." He may be cussing me out in Spanish for all I know.

He notices the ocean book on my lap. "I see you've been raiding my bookshelves."

"Sorry, but I figured I should read up."

He waves it off. "Help yourself to any of my books."

"Okay, thanks." Now I don't feel so bad about creeping around his office.

"Based on your reading," he says, "if you were an oceanographer, what animal would you study?"

Definitely not the creepy eel lurking in my dreams. "Maybe something bizarre like the oarfish or viperfish."

He laughs. "The oarfish lives so deep under the ocean you'd have to practically live undersea for years to study them." He takes another sip. "The viperfish is interesting, though."

"Yeah?"

"It looks like something out of a horror movie. Its jaws are wider than its body and can open to a 90-degree angle to bite prey larger than itself. Its teeth look like rakes."

"Have you ever seen one?"

"Not in person. They only rise to the surface at night. If you're ever in the ocean at night and you see a little blue light, it could be a viperfish."

"Do they try to eat humans?"

"Not that I'm aware. We're too big and we don't taste like fish."

I scratch a few notes on my notepad.

He studies me. "If you're still around here in the fall, I'll see if I can get you on the San Juan dive."

"In Puerto Rico?"

"No, the San Juan Islands here in Washington. It's a graduate workshop for science and poetry majors." He drains his glass. "But I have connections."

So, he *does* want me to stay. "That sounds perfect for my portfolio project." I swig from my nearly full wineglass to try and keep up with my father.

He reaches for his empty glass and sets it back down. He shouts toward the kitchen. "Jenny bear, is there any wine left?"

"Coming!" she replies.

I look at my next question. "You said turtles feed on jellyfish, but as turtles decrease in number, jellyfish increase and become a problem. How?"

"They kill salmon and eat the larvae of fish. Jellies also eat the plankton that fish eat, so fish are literally starving to death. Plus, about a thousand people a day are stung by jellies."

I scan through my questions. "What does a jellyfish sting feel like?"

He lifts the lighter from the table and snaps on the flame. "Give me your arm. I'll show you."

"Uh, no, I think I'm good." He chuckles and sets the lighter down. "Are they poisonous?"

"All of them emit poisonous venom," he says, "but most are not deadly. Usually a sting hurts for a few hours, but there's no permanent damage."

"Have you been stung?"

"Oh yeah. One does not work in the ocean and not suffer bites, cuts, and stings." He shows me his arms and legs pocked with small compressions and scars. He lifts his shirt and reveals a long scar on his back.

"Wow, did you get speared by a shark?"

He releases his shirt. "No, *this* one is from not clearing the boat in time. I got caught on the rope hook."

I recoil. "How about the scar on the back of your hand?"

He examines it. "Got bit by a turtle."

"A sea turtle?"

He shakes his head. "Back in high school a couple of buddies and I were traipsing around the woods and we came upon a snapper. I picked him up." He gazes at the back of his hand again. "He didn't like it much."

"Lucky you didn't lose the hand. How'd you get the turtle off?"

He winces. "One of my friends pulled out his Swiss Army knife and decapitated it." He taps the empty glass. "I always felt bad about that. But my buddy saved my hand."

I flip the notebook to a new page. "So what samples do you collect from the ocean?"

"Depends. On this last trip to Pacific Beach we collected sediment samples."

"What were you looking for?"

"Pollution. Radioactivity."

"Radioactivity? In the water?"

"We're still finding radioactive material from the Japan tsunami. We'll be picking up tsunami debris on the beaches and in the ocean for years. But there are other sources."

"Of radioactivity?"

"That, and junk in general."

I cringe. "You write a lot about the plastics in the ocean," I say. "You said 80% of the ocean contains plastic. Has there been any progress on cleaning it up?"

"Some, like the 4ocean project. But plastics are like a drug resistant virus."

"In what way?"

"Unlike paper, plastic doesn't biodegrade. When you throw it away, it may crumble, but it doesn't fully disappear." He yells toward the house. "Did you hear that, Jen?"

She tips across the lawn carrying a fresh bottle of wine. "I'm not ready to give up my bottled water."

He points to me. "You're about twenty percent plastic."

"I am?"

"It's inside processed food and beverages, synthetic fabrics, soaps, shampoos. It's even in junk food wrappers."

Jennifer sets the bottle down. "Why are you scaring Michael with your statistics?"

My father kisses her hand. "He started it."

"I kind of did," I say.

155

Laura Moe

She knocks on top of my head. "Be careful what you ask for."

"Thanks for the wine, my love," my father says. "Care to join us?"

"No, this looks like a boys' club." She curtsies and heads back inside the house.

I'm not sure I'm ready to know, but I ask my next question. "Is it true that by 2050 there will be more plastic in the ocean than fish?"

He pours us each a fresh glass of wine. "Now the estimate is by 2035. Maybe sooner."

My heart thumps as if I've sprinted a mile. "Can we do anything about it?"

"Not much at this point. Too many people in the government think our scientific evidence is hokum. And the plastics industry itself lobbies against laws to place controls on it." He sighs. "Originally, plastic was a great invention, but too much of a good thing creates an imbalance. Between the NRA, the junk food industry, pesticides, and plastics, we're creating our own extinction."

He picks up the lighter. "I find hundreds of these things on the beaches. Jen and I should use matches, but you have to admit, these gadgets come in handy, so it's hard not to be hypocritical. I avoid plastic bottles, bags, and containers, but some things slip through the cracks."

"In Ohio we pretty much throw everything away."

"It takes work, but if we want to save the planet, we all need to be willing to pay more, own less, and leave a smaller footprint." He fiddles with the lighter. "I purposely

156

paid more for this because it *is* refillable. I use refillable ballpoint pens, too, but the pens and the refills themselves are also made of plastic."

Jennifer pokes her head out the door. "Are you two good with just salad and cold cuts for dinner?"

My father and I exchange a look and nod. "That sounds great, babe," he tells her. He looks at me. "What else do you want to know?"

"I did some research about that 4ocean group. They've been successful."

He cocks his head. "Those guys have designed a collaborative, economic means to solve this issue. Their work is innovative and cost effective, and I think someday they'll win a Nobel Prize."

"Do you ever hope to win a Nobel Prize?"

He chuffs. "I wouldn't turn one down, but the work itself is the reward."

"I think a lot of writers feel that way, too."

There's a relaxed crevice in the conversation, and we both quietly enjoy our wine and the yellow summer evening. He leans forward and ruffles through Jack's fur. "Overall, what have you learned in your research?"

"That our planet is fucked."

He barks a loud laugh. "What will you do with this insight?"

I shrug. "Fiction is kind of my forte. I should email my creative nonfiction teacher Frank Barnes and ask what he recommends."

"I know Frank. He's a good writer."

"You do?"

"Sure. He's on my paintball squad."

My mouth drops open. "You play paintball?"

"Even we stodgy old professors have lives." My father regards me with fondness and curiosity, the universal language of a father and son.

It's the look I've waited for my whole life.

Chapter Sixteen

There's a letter sitting on the counter when I come down to breakfast.

"You've got mail." Jennifer says, as she scans through a pile of envelopes and magazines. I hadn't thought to check the mailbox while they were gone.

The return address is from my brother's father. I've never known Paul to be much of a letter writer. Not that he's illiterate. His smarts are more of the common-sense, mechanical variety. The envelope is thick and bears extra postage. I slit it open. A short note on the back of a receipt is attached.

Michael, your mother asked me to mail this for her. She said she doesn't want to know Ashton Meadow's address, so if you reply, send the letter to me and I will make sure she gets it. Hope you're enjoying Seattle.

-Paul

The other envelope contains several sheets of lined notebook paper in my mother's curly handwriting. Some sections are crossed out. There's also a folded rectangle of yellowed paper inside.

I fill a coffee mug. "I think I'll read this outside."

Dear Michael,

Paul told me the real reason you went to Seattle. I was hopping mad at first, but after a couple of days I kind of settled down. I still don't like it. You're invading my past. But Paul is on your side. He says that boys need to know their fathers. And now you have this chance. And he says

159

Ashton Meadows is entitled to know you. So… I have to let it go.

Since you haven't come home, I assume you're staying with him. I don't want to know anything about him or what you two do together. He was always good to me, and you came from our relationship. I'm not dumb enough to think he and I have any sort of future. He only exists in my flawed memory. And I want to hold onto the image of him looking at me as if I was the most beautiful girl he'd ever seen.

In your old bedroom I found a love note your father wrote. It was inside a book he gave me. Voyage to the Bottom the Sea. I never read the book, but I read the note over and over. It's all bent up now and the ink is smeared. I'm sending it to you with this letter because I'm letting it go. Among other things.

Yes. You heard that right. Paul got me to pitch some stuff. It's slow. It's not easy to throw out my entire life. But maybe most of it should be tossed. So much of my life is trash. Being trash. Being loved by men who treated me like trash. Paul was the only who didn't. But I realized that too late.

This shrink Paul made me go to is very patient. She helped me see that the world won't collapse around me if I let some things go.

Like you kids. I've let each of you go one way or another. Jeff still stops by, but he has his own life now. Annie lives with Earl. And you ran clear across the country away from me.

My brother Gil and I never knew our father either. He took off when I was two. Did I ever tell you that? Maybe I told you kids too many fairy tales to protect you from the truth. Or to keep myself from remembering all the men my mother dragged home, all the men who thought they could use me the way a little girl should never be used. Those men! Different names and faces but the same intentions. They would come to my room ~~and rub their hands over my skin and there was one when I was twelve and he did things I can't write here,~~ *things I never wanted my children to know what can happen to a person. Things that may explain why I'm a little crazy.*

My mother had to know why I cried every time she needed rent or drugs and she brought home a new 'uncle.' But she never stopped it. Some men came with toys and candy. Likely to keep me and Gil busy while they were in mom's bedroom. And sometimes they would come looking for me, sometimes both me and Gil.

I stopped looking at their faces and bodies. Only their hands. Dirt under the nails mostly. Scars. Hairy knuckles. Sometimes sun burnt. Calluses that scratched my skin like sandpaper.

If it weren't for Gil, I might be dead. He finally got old enough to fight for both of us. One time he swung a lamp and bashed one of the creeps in the head. Our mother started doing her business elsewhere.

When Gil died my soul died with him, so maybe I don't have enough left of me to be a decent mother.

I never wanted you to know any of this. But the past has a way of sneaking through the back door. It sits and stares at me every time I smell a familiar odor or a song reminds me of a moment. Some good, some bad. Like the other day I recognized the hands of one of the patients in the rehab center. I forget faces, but not hands. He had an X tattoo over each knuckle and a crazy ass pinky finger that looked like it had been stomped by an elephant. And I remembered his raspy old voice. I had to tell the head nurse why I can't go into that man's room if they want him left alive a minute longer. I said, "Don't give me a pair of scissors or I'll snip his IV and let him choke on his own vomit." I'm working the other side of the hall now.

I'm still wearing the cast. The one good thing about having a broken arm is I don't have to do bed pan duty because I can't lift the patients with one arm. I can still change sheets and deliver meals. It just takes me twice as long. And talking to the patients doesn't take two working arms. I can do that blindfolded.

Even if you decide to stay with your father I hope you will come to visit. Eventually your old bedroom will be cleaned out.

It's dark inside my head most of the time. You kids are my light. Paul and Bob taught me how to be as much of a mother as I'm able, and I do love all of you. And I'm proud of you and Jeff for getting your diplomas.

Earl and Annie stopped by the other day to check on me. Annie didn't say much.

Maybe I'm a shitty mother, but I've always loved you kids. ALWAYS. Even when it didn't seem like it. I never wanted you and Jeff and Annie to grow up feeling unloved the way I did.

Love, Mom

Her letter is an arrow through my heart. I refold it and stare at the back fence through watery eyes.

Jack's Cat jumps on my lap and purrs. "Hey, buddy." I stroke his back and he curls onto my thighs.

The note inside the envelope reeks of Mom's house. The odor should repulse me; instead, memories of all three of us kids together flood into my brain. Not every day was a massacre.

The handwriting on my father's note is bold.

Dear S.

I hope you are having a good day. My day always gets brighter third period when you and I meet for tutoring. Before then, it's as if I sleep walk through life until you're near me.

I like to imagine us together driving off to California in my red mustang. The windows rolled down and the wind blowing through your long blonde hair. You smile at me and the world disappears.

See you fifth period!

Love, A.M.

"Holy shit," I mutter. Reading about my father in Mom's diary is one thing, but this letter proves their relationship wasn't one sided. He *did* care about her.

I stash the note and my mother's letter back in the envelope as if they're on fire. My coffee has grown cold, so I step inside to reheat it in the microwave.

"Good news from home?" Jennifer asks.

I sit across from her at the breakfast bar. "In a way. My mother is cleaning up some things." I'm not ready to discuss the rest of the letter.

Jennifer reaches over and gives my hand a squeeze. "That's' wonderful." She shows me something on her iPad from the *Seattle Times*. "Here's another piece of good news. Look who's speaking at The Moore Theatre next week. The show is sold out."

I read aloud, "World renowned ocean scientist and UW faculty member Dr. Ashton Meadows will be addressing strategies for combating global climate change. Copies of his new book, *Man's War with the Ocean*, will be available for sale." I pass the tablet back to her. "Wow. He really *is* famous."

She sets the iPad on the counter. "You should invite Peri to join us."

"I will. I'm meeting her in a few minutes."

When I go upstairs to retrieve my backpack, I hide Mom's letter in the side pocket. Up until this year I was angry at my mother for denying me access to my father. Now I'm just sad for her.

As I walk to Peri's, I slow my pace, pull out my phone, and punch up my mother's number. "Mom?"

She takes a second to respond. "Michael?" She replies in her smoky voice.

"I read your letter." Silence hangs between us like a low cloud. My voice grows spindly. "Mom, I'm so sorry for all the things that happened to you."

She's still on the line because I hear her breathe. "Thank you, sweetheart."

"And you're not a shitty mom. I never felt unloved. Ever."

"You kids are the best things to happen to me." She coughs, and after a long pause, she says, "Are you having a good time out there?"

"I am. I learned a lot in the workshop and made some friends." I describe some of the places I've been, strategically not mentioning my father or Jennifer. "How's the arm?"

"The damn cast itches like crazy, but I can still go to work and drive."

I duck to avoid a cluster of leaves. "Did you get your car fixed? Jeff told me your old one died."

"Paul got me another one."

"What make and model?"

"Hell if I know," she says "It's blue."

"Mom!" I sputter a laugh.

My mother takes a long inhale of her cigarette. "Paul talked me into letting someone come in and help me organize some things."

"Holy crap, Mom! That's great news."

"Maybe for the rest of you." She puffs from her cigarette again.

Two birds on a branch above me share today's news with one another. "Well, Mom, I just wanted to call and thank you for the letter... and to tell you I love you."

"I love you, too, Buttercup."

Buttercup. The last time she called me that was when Bob was still alive.

We chat for a couple more minutes and sign off when I approach Peri's house. Our short conversation both crushes and fulfills me.

Mrs. Diamandis answers the door and tells me to go ahead and meet Peri in the kitchen.

"You're just in time," Peri says. "I'm baking a cake for my dad."

Peri pulls the beaters from her mixer and hands one to me. "Taste."

I lick from the chocolate covered beater. "Ummmm. This is heaven."

"Just wait until I make the frosting."

As the cake bakes, Peri and I take a stroll in her neighborhood. I consider telling her about the letter and note, but she doesn't know the whole story about my mother. Only Shelly does.

"The swashbuckler is speaking at The Moore Theatre next Thursday. Do you want to go?"

She squeezes my hand. "I'd love to."

"I kind of figured you would. Him being your boyfriend and all." My phone buzzes as we walk. I glance at the caller. "It's Dale."

"From the bookstore?"

I nod and poke the green button. "Hey, Dale."

"Are you still interested in a job? It's temporary, but life itself is temporary, and this means you won't die broke."

Chapter Seventeen

Dear Shelly,

As you can see, I'm still here in Seattle. In fact, I'm working with Dale at the university. I don't work *directly* with Dale, but he helped me get hired as a temporary custodian. Essentially, I'm part of a crew of ex-cons and homeless dudes getting the dorms ready for when students come back for fall quarter. All that community service with Earl proved beneficial, especially since I used him as a reference. The hours are irregular, anywhere from twenty to forty hours a week, but it pays twelve bucks an hour, which, in Rooster, is a king's ransom. Plus, I get paid at the end of each shift.

So, I was just arriving home from a full day of sanitizing dorm rooms at the university last night when my father's wife Jennifer called out to me from the kitchen.

"I'm headed out to the book club to discuss *Kafka on the Shore.* You're welcome to join us. I'd love to hear your input."

Kafka on the Shore is by the same guy who wrote *Norwegian Wood.* You should check this one out. It's about a kid who calls himself Kafka and runs away from home to find his missing mother and sister. The book resonates with me because I relate to Kafka Tamura. Not that I ran away from home, but I left home to find parts of my missing family. And you did the same thing when you ran off to San Francisco.

Anyway, as Jennifer and I headed out the front door, my father yelled from behind his desk. "Have fun, *ladies*." I was ready to give him the finger, but Jennifer beat me to it.

Jennifer's book club meets in the back room of a brew pub in Ballard. Jennifer said the pub didn't mind if we brought in food as long as each of us ordered two drinks. I asked for a beer and no one questioned my age. Just in case, I had Michael Neruda's license with me.

There were about a dozen women, some old, others closer to Jennifer's age. I was the only guy, but Jennifer told them who I was and why I was there.

As we ate, the group leader asked questions about the book, and the ladies went around the room and stated their opinions.

One woman said it reminded her of the magical realism of Gabriel Garcia Marquez's work. Another said this book was a retelling of Oedipus.

Jennifer pulled out a photocopied sheet. "According to Murakami, you have to read this novel more than once to solve its many riddles."

"Well, it made no sense to me," one woman crowed. "The man who could talk to cats was a wacky storyline. And what was all that business with Colonel Sanders and Johnnie Walker?"

Up to this point I hadn't commented, so all eyes turned to me when I said, "I think those are metaphors. They make a statement about modern consumerism and how we are seduced by instant gratification."

The ladies all looked at me as if I were a rock star. And then I added, "I think it's just a book you have to read and savor, but not over-analyze. Great books take you inside a different world and let you linger there, and when you're finished you come out blinking like the lights are too bright."

Jennifer beamed at me, so I knew I scored huge points.

I think you'd like the book. My favorite line in it is, "metaphors can reduce the distance." It's why great poets like Pablo Neruda make us pay attention to everyday things. They reduce the distance so we can understand things we may not consciously understand.

I'm still trying to discover a metaphor for us. A tsunami perhaps, where the sea pulls further and further back until it returns and wallops everything in its path.

Anyway, the women invited me back. So now I'm part of a ladies' book club.

But there's more. As we filed out of the back room, I heard a familiar voice.

Theo.

He sat facing me in a booth halfway through the bar. I glanced around for a rear exit just as he noticed me. My first thought was, *what would Shelly do*? You'd make me march up and say hello to him like you did when I kept trying to avoid my ex-friend Rick.

Theo waved me over, and Jennifer asked if I knew him.

"That's Theo," I said.

I had told her about you, Theo, and the whole calamity. I'm well over it. Just as you told me to, I moved on.

Jennifer leaned in, and said, "Well, he's seen you, so you can't escape now." She nudged me toward the booth where he sat across from his blonde poet girlfriend.

Theo stood up. He tried to give me a hug, but I backed away. "Michael, you remember Flora?" He gestured to the blonde.

I shook her hand, and introduced Jennifer.

"Would you like to join us?" Theo asked.

Jennifer and I exchanged a glance. She appeared curious, yet, unlike you, who would have grabbed my shirt and flung me into the booth, Jennifer let me decide.

"We can spare a minute or two." I sat next to Flora and Jennifer slid in beside Theo.

After an awkward silence, Theo said, "Dale tells me you're cleaning dorms at the U."

"Yep."

"Have you been writing?"

I shrugged. "A little."

After another tense silence, Theo raised his beer glass. "Flora and I are celebrating. Her book just got accepted at Penguin."

I turned to face her. "That's awesome. Is it a poetry collection?"

"No, it's a novel."

I thought it must be killing Theo, a fiction writer, that his *poet* girlfriend has a novel coming out with a big publisher. But he didn't seem jealous. Maybe he'd already drunk a shitload of beer.

Then Flora said, "We're also celebrating Theo's dissertation and defense being accepted." She raised her glass. "He's now officially Dr. Garibaldi."

"Congratulations to both of you," Jennifer said.

So, there I was, celebrating the success of one of my betrayers, and now I'm telling the tale to my other betrayer.

I click SEND

Chapter Eighteen

The Moore Theatre buzzes with conversation. Jennifer, Peri, and I sit in front row balcony seats. It's cool to be treated like a VIP. Jennifer bought me a new shirt and dress pants. She also paid for a haircut. I snap a selfie and text it to Shoe. He texts back. *-Not bad for a straight guy.*

The lights dim and the crowd powers down. After a brief introduction, my father strides across the stage as if he owns it, not bothered that almost two thousand people are gawking at him. He stands at the podium and scans the auditorium. He appears more relaxed in front of this roomful of strangers than in his own home.

My father wraps his fingers along each side of the podium and bows toward the audience. He waits for the applause to die down. "Thank you. Thank you so much. I'm grateful for this opportunity to speak to you tonight about the realities of global warming." A vivid image of multicolored fish and coral materializes behind him on a giant screen.

"As a graduate student in the 90's, I had the opportunity to be part of a dive team off the coast of Australia. We came upon this reef, emblazoned with bold colors and teeming with life, as if the fish and turtles were celebrating their own Mardi Gras."

He pauses, and clicks to the next slide, which shows mud-colored plant life. "I had no idea when I visited the same reef ten years later, that coral would turn brown."

There's a gasp from the audience. "In a single decade, in place of the gaudy fish and lively green turtles, this body of water was populated by jellyfish, plankton, and dead coral."

He walks away from the podium and crosses the stage. "Environmental change is natural, but the accelerating decrease in size and population of megafauna is cause for alarm. Whales dying from starvation, turtles suffocating on plastic bags, fish dying from lack of oxygen, and seals choking on fibers in fishing nets are not naturally occurring events.

"Every action we make affects the ecosystem. Each time we toss out a plastic fork or bottle, we change the ocean's composition." He gestures to the slide. "The consequences are alarming and evident."

He lifts a water bottle at the podium and frowns. "My wife's argument for these bottles is they are an easy and convenient delivery system. She tends to lose the expensive glass and stainless-steel bottles, so she justifies using disposable by cost."

He pauses, glances our way, and blows her a kiss. "I love you, honey." The audience laughs.

"Yet there's a high price for this convenience. Just as the dollar menu at McDonald's seems like a short range, economical way to feed yourself, in the long run, the burden of cost outweighs convenience. A diet of hydrogenated fats, sugar, and empty calories will lead to heart problems, weight gain, and an early death."

He raises the plastic bottle again. "The long-range cost of our addiction to convenience is we are killing our oceans. Not only are plastics and other debris accumulating on the ocean's surface and affecting flora and fauna, these elements are changing the chemical properties of water itself."

My father sets the bottle down, steeples his fingers, and rests his elbows on the podium. "If we want to save our planet, we need to change how we live, and we need to begin yesterday...."

Jennifer leans toward me. "See that man at the podium?" She squeezes my hand. "He's going to get lucky tonight."

"Even after he publicly trashed you?"

She rubs her palms together. "I might have to use the whips and chains on him for that."

***

After my father's speech, Jennifer, Peri, and I walk down to meet him in the lobby. It's crowded, and we don't find him right away. When Jennifer spots him, my father is talking to a reporter from KOMO news. There are too many people around him to get close, so we wait.

The reporter ends her interview and my father is swallowed up by a large cluster of protesters wearing red T-shirts emblazoned with *Skeptics of Science* on the front. One woman raises a poster that says, GLOBAL WARMING IS A HOAX! Others carry signs reading, ANIMALS AND PLANTS CAN ADAPT. Other signs say, THE EARTH IS A-OKAY, CHANGE IS NATURAL, SCIENTISTS ARE LYING TO YOU!

Several bystanders shove their way in to hold up their phones and record as the protestors march in a circle around my father. The sign carriers shout in unison, "Global warming is a hoax!"

I glance at Jennifer. "Is he going to be okay?"

"Those idiots show up at every event. They're not violent, just creepy."

The cameraman from the news station aims his lens on the scene. My father nods at the *Skeptics of Science.* "Thank you for coming tonight. I appreciate that you have your own opinions."

"They're not opinions!" The guy in the front of the group moves in closer to him. "They're facts! *You're* the liar!"

My father grins. "Feel lucky to live in a country where it is legal to openly express your views."

Another guy, wearing a red ball cap, gets in my father's face. "It's tree huggers like you that are ruining this country!"

I pull forward to defend my father, but Jennifer holds me back. "He'll be fine. He's used to this."

"Seriously?"

"The first time I saw this I was afraid, too, but Ash is one cool customer."

My father stands with his legs planted in an inverted V, his arms crossed at his chest, a faint smile resting on his lips, as if he welcomes the confrontation.

A pair of security guards hustles the group to the exit. As they walk out, one of the protestors raises his fist, and shouts, "He's making stuff up to sell books! Ashton Meadows is a liar! Don't buy his lies!"

The group chants "Global warming is a hoax!" as they recede toward the street.

A woman escorts my father to an oblong table stacked with books where a long line of people waits to have them signed. An armed security guard stands behind him.

Jennifer looks at Peri and me. "Ash is going to be here at least an hour. You two don't have to wait around."

"I have to work early tomorrow, anyway," Peri says.

Peri and I sift our way through a gathering of protestors and counter-protestors outside The Moore. We take the bus to her parents' house, where we are coerced into watching some cop show TV. When the show ends, Peri says, "We need to switch to KOMO news. Michael's father will be on."

He's one of the lead stories. News footage depicts a skirmish that occurred after Peri and I left. One of the SOS bashed one of my father's supporters with his sign. People on both sides started a scuffle before the cops broke them up.

"We should have hung around longer," Peri says. "We missed all the action."

"That ought to help your father sell a few books," Mr. Diamandis says.

My father and Jennifer are still up when I arrive home around midnight. They sit side by side on the couch, Jennifer's feet tucked under her butt. She holds a flute of champagne. Jazz emanates from the awesome sound system in my father's office. A copy of my father's aqua-blue book sits on the coffee table next to his glass of champagne.

I settle into an adjacent chair. "Aren't you old folks up way past your bed time?"

He grins. "I'm too keyed up to sleep. I met some fantastic people while signing books. Their interest in my work gives me hope for the planet."

"You were on the news tonight. A couple of people got arrested."

"A little drama helps sell books." He sips his champagne.

"That's what Peri's dad said."

Jennifer offers to pour me some champagne but I shake my head. I turn to my father. "It was a great speech."

"It was!" Jennifer says. "Even though Ash dragged my reputation through the mud." She gives him a friendly punch. They kiss, and I look away.

Jennifer refills her glass. "Your father is also speaking at the Save the Planet Gala this Saturday night."

"Is it a big party?"

"It's huge!" Jennifer gestures and dribbles champagne on her wrist. "It's being held on the top floor of The Columbia Tower. Famous people will be there. Bill and Melinda Gates... the mayor and the governor ... and who else, hon?"

"A bunch of writers and musicians...like Bono and Deb Caletti," he says.

My father is partying with Bono?

Jennifer reaches for my father's face and pouts. "And then his international book tour begins, and I won't see my sweetie for weeks."

He kisses her fingers. "We'll be together for some of it."

Jennifer looks at me. "We're going to London, Paris, and Berlin. But then I have to be back when school starts." She pouts again. "He's going to Italy without me."

"Wow. You're kind of like the Mick Jagger of ocean science."

He chuckles. "The tour isn't as glamorous as it sounds. I spend most of it drinking coffee, trying to figure out what day and time it is."

"Anyway," Jennifer slurs, "we'll be out again Saturday night, so if you and Peri want to hang around here, you'll have the house to yourselves." She winks at me.

"Okay."

"We would have invited you," my father says, "but it's a closed, ticketed event, and tickets were distributed six months ago."

And he didn't know me six months ago.

He sets his glass down and reaches for the book on the coffee table. "I autographed this for Peri. I hope I've spelled her name right." He pushes his book toward me.

"Great. Thanks." I stand and pick up the book. "I think I'll head up to bed. I have to be up early to clean dorms."

As I walk up the steps it hits me; I am my mother's son. My famous father is way out of my league.

Chapter Nineteen

I'm still half asleep when my phone buzzes. I roll over to ignore whoever is texting me. It buzzes again. And again. And again. I groan and reach over to pick it up. Shelly's name lights up the screen. It's been almost two months since I last spoke to her. I sit up and read the messages.

-*Neruda!*

-*Are you up?*

-*Hey, it's me!*

-*I got your email!*

What email? Oh shit. I sent that one.

What did I say in my message that made her want to contact me at 6:15 in the morning? Right. It's 9:15 in Ohio.

I drag my body up and head to the bathroom.

As the shower water hits my face, I recall writing about the book club. And Theo. Ugh. He's like a giant cockroach I can't step on. When the world ends, it will be full of cockroaches, plastic bottles, and Theo.

My mind drifts back to the moment in late June when my father finally contacted me. I needed to tell someone. The one person who cared the most, of course, was Shelly. But after the mess with Theo, I blocked her number. I've since unblocked her, but I had cut her from my life.

Until I sent that stupid email.

Why can't I admit to myself that she and I are over? I shut the shower off and towel myself dry.

When I come down at 6:30, Jennifer is in the kitchen. She glances at me. "You're up early."

I pour a cup of coffee and reach for a banana. "Today's my last day as a temporary custodian at the university."

"That's been a good job for you, hasn't it?"

"It has. I enjoy cleaning stuff." I scoot onto the stool across from her. "How late were you guys up celebrating?"

She sets her iPad down and yawns. "We went to bed shortly after you did."

"Is he going to be back from his speaking tour when the quarter starts?"

"Ash is only advising this term," Jennifer says. "He doesn't have to be back until October for the San Juan trip."

I pull the skin back on the banana. "He asked me to go with him on that."

Jennifer reaches over and pats my hand. "I'm so happy you two found common ground. You know, if you really want to go to the ball tomorrow night, you can use my ticket."

I bite into the banana and consider this. A chance to meet Bill Gates and Bono? That would be cool. But would my father be comfortable explaining just who the hell I am? Even though things are good between us now, he still hasn't publicly acknowledged me. "Thanks anyway, but I think I'll pass."

"If it's a matter of clothing, I'm sure Ash will loan you a suit."

I swallow the rest of the banana and dump my peel in the compost bin under the sink. "No. This is your big Hollywood moment. You get to be the famous author's eye candy."

She gives me a hug, which tells me she's glad I turned down her offer.

I grab a second banana and head out to catch the bus. At the bus stop, I reread Shelly's texts. Should I text her back?

She always made me wait.

I've enjoyed being a sub custodian. There's something therapeutic about wiping away debris. Maybe it's a metaphor for erasing messy moments from my past.

The work itself reminds me of last summer's community service with Shelly. It's probably time for me leave her in the past, too.

At the end of my shift, I collect my last pay envelope and walk to the art building to model for Peri's drawing group again.

Two buildings away from my destination I spot my father. My first instinct is to approach him, but he's not alone. He's standing in the entrance of Smith Hall laughing with a female student.

I step behind a tree and watch. She places her hand on my father's forearm and keeps it there. He says something to her, she nods, they embrace, and she disappears inside the building.

With a smile on his face, he strides toward the parking garage.

My heart thumps. What the hell was that? Maybe it's innocent. And it's not like he kissed her. But still. They were awfully cozy.

I wait for my heart rate to calm, and then cut across the quad to the art building.

Standing naked in a room full of others is easier this time. Partly because I know what to expect, and partly because I'm distracted by seeing my father with that girl.

But it was out in the open and people know him here. It has to be innocent.

Sometimes I wish I could switch off my overactive imagination.

After drawing, Peri and I stop at the coffee shop again. This time I just order coffee and a peanut butter cookie.

"Earth to Michael," she says.

"What?"

"You seem kind of out of it today."

"It was my last day of work." I can't tell her about what I saw in front of Smith Hall, or Shelly's texts.

"I enjoyed your father's presentation last night."

Just mentioning him kinks up my insides, but I reach into my bag and pull out his book. "The swashbuckler autographed this for you."

She presses it against her heart.

I roll my eyes. "Did he spell your name right?"

She flips it open. "No, but it's okay. Nobody does." She shows me. He spelled it Pere. "Is he making any more speeches soon?"

He's the last person I want to talk about. I snap my cookie in half and take a bite. "He's setting out on an international speaking tour in a couple of weeks."

She pages through the book. "Sounds exciting."

"He claims it isn't. Jennifer's going to be with him for part of it."

"That means you'll have the house to yourself again?"

"Seems that way."

Peri gives me a little smile. "I'll try to keep you from getting too bored."

I arch my eyebrows. "I'm counting on it."

Chapter Twenty

My father is reading a newspaper at the counter when I come down for breakfast. He and I nod at one another and I pour myself a cup of coffee.

"I've never seen you guys read an actual newspaper," I say.

He closes the paper. "Jenny bought a few copies this morning because there's a story about the confrontation and a review of my speech."

"I hope it's a good review."

"It is." He slides an extra paper toward me. "Jen tells me you've never been to the ocean."

"Not yet."

He glances at the clock. "It's only 7:30. If you're game, we can drive to Pacific Beach and be back this afternoon."

"Isn't your big party tonight?"

He shrugs. "It's not until eight. A round trip is seven hours."

"Okay."

"Wear long pants," my father says. "And bring a jacket. It'll be chilly there."

I run up the steps two at a time. My father has just asked to spend the entire day with me. Just him and me.

After I change clothes and come back down, Jennifer hands me a tote bag containing snacks. She kisses my father. "You boys behave. And be back in time."

"Are we bringing Jack?" I ask.

"Sorry guys," Jennifer says. "The dogs have an appointment with the groomer today."

We pick up the ferry in Edmonds to Kingston. Once on board, we climb to the top deck. "I like making this trip on a clear day when the mountains are out." He points to the right. "That's Mount Baker, and to our left is Mount Rainier."

I snap a photo of each, and I'm tempted to ask my father to pose for a selfie with me, but he wanders off toward the front of the ferry. I take a picture of him in profile as he pitches against the railing to gaze at the horizon.

Standing next to him, I wonder if others see us as a father and son enjoying a weekend outing together.

I text Peri. -*Swashbuckler and I are going to the ocean together*!!!!

I raise my phone and sneak a picture of him in the background behind me. His face is somewhat blurry, but the resemblance between us is clear. I text that to Peri, too.

A couple approaches him. The woman holds out a copy of my father's book and asks for an autograph. I snap a photo.

Once we reach land, we cruise through remote areas on two-lane, narrow highways that wind up and down. The drive reminds me of back roads near Rooster, and I wonder if my father notices the similarities. According to a highway sign it's more than a hundred miles to Pacific

Beach. This will be a long-ass drive unless one of us starts talking. "Do you miss living in Ohio?"

He glances at me, takes his time formulating a reply. "There are aspects of it I miss. When my brother and I were kids we had all sorts of adventures."

"Like what?"

"We lived on a lake, and we spent our summers swimming, or on our rowboat. Ed built the boat with his best friend. Sometimes he and I took it out on nearby rivers and went camping."

"Sounds like me and Jeff. Except we had an old canoe that Paul fixed up for us."

"Jeff is Susan and Paul's son?"

I nod. "He looks like a younger version of Paul without the mullet."

My father laughs. "The nineties were a bad, bad time for fashion. Big hair and shoulder pads on girls, bad sweaters and Duran Duran hair on guys." He stares at the road ahead. "One of the things I liked about your mother is she didn't follow a trend. She was just herself."

My mom didn't have the money to follow trends, but I don't say this. Even if Mom could afford to, she would create her own trends. "Did she ever get to ride in your red Mustang?"

He rubs at his bristly chin. "Yeah. I think I drove her to work a couple of times. She worked at Burger King near the mall."

"Yeah, she wrote about that in her journal. She hated the brown polyester uniform. Said it made her look like a Browns fan."

He chuckles. "Thank God I never had the time or the need to work a nametag job."

"Even when you were in college?"

"My tuition and dorm were paid for. I tutored math and science during my undergrad days for spending money. A lot of math idiots make it into college."

"Count me part of that group."

He looks over and gives me a thin smile. "If you hang around here and go to U dub, I can help you with the math stuff."

"Thanks. But I plan to major in English."

"You still need basic math and science courses no matter what you major in."

"I might already have those. I took all college classes last year through Post-secondary options. My principal and counselor thought it would be better for Shelly and me to finish senior year off campus."

"Who's Shelly?"

My face reddens. "My ex-girlfriend. I met her while doing community service."

He nods. "Yes. Jen mentioned her. Sounds like you two had a bad break up."

I'm weirded out that Jennifer and my father discussed my love life. I wonder how much he knows. "Yeah."

"Well, you seemed to have moved on."

"I have."

I consider showing him the note he wrote to my mother long ago, but we start talking about dogs, running, and music, and the moment passes.

We stop for lunch at a cafe in Aberdeen and eat fish 'n chips. He chomps down on a slab of battered fish. "Don't tell Jen I'm eating fried food."

Back on the road, he drives west toward Pacific Beach. A half hour later, we reach a Research Access sign, and he turns there. He parks the Subaru along the road. "Not many people come here because there aren't any facilities. It's a good location for my team to work without interruption. The only problem is when a corpse washes up on shore."

"Does that happen?" I ask.

"Might be a good place to dump a body since it's so remote." He grins. "I'm kidding."

"Oh. Okay." It crosses my mind he could easily kill me while we're here. As a scientist he'd know how to cover his tracks.

He wasn't kidding about it being cooler here than Seattle, so I pull on my hoodie as we begin our walk. We trek through about a quarter of a mile of dense reeds toward the sound of waves. The sky is a forlorn gray.

We reach a clearing at the end of the tall reeds and stop. Except for a handful of Black-bellied Plovers, the beach is deserted.

He spreads his hands. "Welcome to my office. What do you think?"

The water crashes violently against the shore and the ground thrums as if we're standing railroad tracks with an approaching train. The wind makes it hard to stand still. I turn toward my father. The waves are so loud I shout, "It's like being inside the eye of a storm."

He squints. "Interesting analogy."

"It feels like the ground is moving," I say.

"It is. The waves are caused by wind, and they come at us with more horsepower than a semi."

How would Neruda describe it? *The sea thunders as if to warn me of its power.* "Are we in danger of a tidal wave?"

"Not at the moment. A Tsunami can happen at any time, but if it happens, we'll get a warning."

A gust blows my hair straight up from my head. I put on my hood and zip up my jacket. "That's some wicked wind."

"Storm's coming in," he says. "It will hit Seattle in a day or so."

I remove my shoes and socks, roll up my jeans, and walk into the waves. The frigid water roils around my feet.

I turn to see if my father's watching, but he crouches over a spot in the sand. He removes his sunglasses, hangs them on his collar, and leans down for closer inspection.

A couple of minutes later I jog back toward my father. "You weren't kidding about the cold. No wonder nobody's swimming."

"Even if it were warm enough to swim today, this isn't a good spot."

"Why not?

"You'd likely get sick." He points to a mass of grayish brown foam in a cove about a quarter mile north of us. "Let's go take a look."

I rub my feet dry and slide my shoes and socks back on. We follow the brown mass as it increases in size. "What is all that?"

"We call it whale sperm."

I scrunch my face. "Is that what it is?"

"There may be some of that in there, but it's mainly debris and other pollutants released into the water. If you look closely enough, you'll notice some of it glistens."

"Because of phosphorescence?"

"Costume glitter. It doesn't bio degrade."

"You mean the kind of glitter cheerleaders glue to posters and tape up all over school?"

He nods. "The very same."

The water in the cove looks like someone poured a bottle of glitter over a chocolate milkshake, except it smells like a sewer.

"This is the part of the ocean we'd like to pretend doesn't exist," he says. "But when we use the sea as a dumping ground, the wreckage ends up resurfacing. Combine that with other pollutants, and the mixture is toxic."

A gust of wind blows my hood off and I stuff my hands in my pockets. "My tenth-grade science teacher said when he was a kid up in Cleveland, Lake Erie used to be flammable. He and his buddies would throw lit matches in the water and watch the flames skim the surface."

Laura Moe

"The EPA did wonders cleaning up that region," he says. "Of course, nowadays, the right-wing politicians believe there's no need for environmental protection."

"How can they not see we're killing the earth?"

He stuffs his hands in his pants pockets and squints into the horizon. "To quote the late, great Aldo Leopold, 'man always kills the thing he loves, so we pioneers have killed the wilderness.'"

A massive wave crashes in and sprays us with drizzle. We stroll along the shore a few more minutes until my father says, "We'd better head home. The wait for the ferry on the way back will be longer since it's the weekend. Jen would kill me if we were late for the Gala."

An hour into the drive back to Seattle, my father announces, "Whoa ho! The old Subaru just turned over 200,000 miles!" He glances at me. "Let's stop for a beer and celebrate."

We pull off the highway at a place called *Bill's*, its neon sign advertising Michelob. My father strides across the lot, and I say, "hey, want to get a snapshot to document the day?"

"Sure."

My father and I stand next to one another in front of the Subaru. I extend my arm and take a selfie of the two of us together.

Chapter Twenty-One

If this hasn't been the best day of my life, it's in the top five. I'm finding the details missing from my life. My mom gave me the half that includes getting me to where I am now. And now my father will help fill in the half that will help determine my future.

Maybe it's a good thing my mother kept my father from me all those years. Maybe I needed to be ready to know him.

I text Peri. -*After today I feel truly connected to him. It sounds dumb to think we drove three hours each way to spend ten minutes on a deserted beach, but it was more about the journey than the destination. Plus, I can now say I've been to the ocean.*

P- *Good!*

The microwave pings. I slide the pasta onto a plate and sit at the breakfast bar when Jennifer strolls in. I whistle. She's a knockout in a low-cut emerald green satin dress. She spins around to give me the full affect.

"I chose green since the theme is saving the planet." She shows me her spiky, black heels. "I'll be taller than Ash tonight."

My father steps in wearing a black tux. Their eyes travel over each other. She flashes him some leg and he growls. She hands me her phone and I snap a few pictures of them. I take a couple with my own phone.

"We're taking Jen's car," he says, "so if you go out, feel free to use mine." He sets his keys on the counter.

Laura Moe

"They're not sending a limo?"

My father chuckles. "I'm not *that* much of a rock star."

After they leave, I text Peri again. *-Here's a photo of the swashbuckler in a tux.*

P-Hot! Suitable for framing!

ME-*Have a car and the house to myself. Want to hang out?*

She doesn't respond, so I guess she's working. The night is supple and warm, so I grab a beer and sit in the back yard with the dogs and a couple of books. I also bring my journal and pens.

It grows too dark to read and the dogs and I venture indoors. I set my books on the breakfast bar and toss a handful of dog treats on the floor. I grab a Kashi Bar for myself. Jack and Lucy scramble for their treats and we saunter into the study. Lucy makes herself comfortable on her dog bed. I sink into one of the leather recliners and flip on the TV, looking forward to binge watching *Port-landia*. Peri told me this show will help me understand the Pacific Northwest.

Jack trots off. I'm about to click on episode One when Jack returns holding his leash in his teeth. "Are you telling me you want to go for a walk?"

He thumps his tail and eyes me. "But it's dark out." Jack continues to stare at me with sad dog eyes.

I sigh. "Okay." I turn off the TV, and clip the leash to his collar, double checking to make sure there are poop bags inside the side pocket. "How about you, Lucy?"

She opens one eye but remains in the bed. I gaze at my father's dog. "I guess it's just you and me, buddy."

I pocket my phone, grab the door keys, and Jack and I set out for a night's walk.

Green Lake closes at dark, so we traipse along sparsely lit sidewalks on Woodlawn. My father's dog appears to be up for a couple of miles.

As Jack and I lumber on, I think about Shelly's text. What would I say to her? Thanks for letting me know you read the email? Of all my real and imaginary notes, what made me send that one? Maybe I wanted her to see I halfway made-up with Theo. His betrayal no longer owns me.

Maybe that's the key to life, you let go of crap so you can move forward. You can't carry the ruins forever. Eventually you have to throw it all away.

Maybe my mother is figuring out that she must toss out all the old garbage so she can begin a new life. The life she deserves.

Jack finds a spot on the grass and does his business. I whisk the poop into one of the bags and tie it shut. We aren't far from Peri's house, so I take us down Ravenna Blvd.

Holding Jack's leash and the dog shit in one hand, I text with the other. -*I'm near your house. Should I stop by?*

A minute later, she replies. -*Sorry. Not home. On a date.*

Me-*WTF? I thought…*

Suddenly the phone is wrenched from my grasp and a fist meets my face. The street spins and I stumble. After a whack in the back of the knee, I collapse and let go of the leash and dog poop. I'm on a merry go round, spiraling round and round, but instead of music, a dog barks. Hands pull my pockets inside out. Two guys wearing hoodies dance around me.

Jack sinks his teeth into one of the dude's legs. "Get him offa me!"

The other guy raises a bat.

"No!" I try to stand, but I'm a beat too late. I hear the crack of wood against bone.

Jack lets go, and the dude yells, "Motherfucker! What is this?"

The guy with the bat laughs "You stepped in dog shit, asshole."

One of them kicks me again, and they dash into the night.

Jack whimpers and tries to get up. "No! Stay." I crawl toward him. His left front leg is bent at an unnatural angle.

I hobble myself up to a squatting position. Forming a stretcher with both arms, I lift Jack and carry him. He's heavy, and I'm a mess, but we can't stay here. It's a slow mile and a half as I stagger us back to the house.

By the time we make it to my father's, I can't see out of my left eye. Grateful there are only two steps to their front door, I gingerly fumble for the key in my pocket. Shit. They took my keys.

Lucy barks and scratches furiously from the other side. I crouch, lay Jack on the stoop, and vomit in the shrubs. I fall against the front door and rest my head against it. I stroke Jack's face to calm him, and Lucy's incessant barking fades to black.

***

The front door swings open and I fall inside. "Oh my God, what happened?" Jennifer says. Out of my good eye I see she's still wearing the shimmering green dress.

My voice comes out in patches. "I was out... walking with Jack...we got mugged. I think they broke Jack's leg."

"What's going on?" My father appears behind her. He sees Jack. "What the hell did you do to my dog?"

"Ash!" Jennifer says.

He removes his tux jacket and wraps it around Jack. He cradles the dog in his arms and carries him inside.

Jennifer helps me stand. "Michael got mugged while he was walking Jack."

My father's eyes bore into me. "Why the hell were you walking around so late at night?"

"He..." A spear of pain in my ribs keeps from me saying more.

"You could have gotten him killed." My father inspects Jack's injuries. "Jen, we need to get him to the vet right away."

"But Michael's hurt, too."

"Jennifer," my father says sharply. "I need you to drive while I hold onto Jack."

"I'll be fine," I croak, leaning on the banister. "Go help Jack."

She mouths, "I'm sorry," and follows my father as he carries his dog toward the garage.

I slowly climb the steps, trying not to yelp from the stabs of pain. By the time I reach the third step, I hear the car peal out of the driveway.

Lucy examines me as I grip the rails and make the slow ascent to my room. I strip in front of the bathroom mirror and look at my bruised self. My left eye is swollen shut. I should have grabbed a bag of ice when I was downstairs, but there's no way I'll make it up and down those steps again.

I let the shower warm up and sidle in. The water stings like fire, but it loosens the blood and I'm able to open my left eye.

It hurts to towel off so I drip dry naked in the bathroom and swallow a handful of aspirin. There are a couple of cans of *Olympia* in my beer fridge. I hold a cold can over my eye. It's a sweet pain, the pain of relief, the kind of pain that reminds me my cells are working in overdrive to heal me.

I usually sleep in boxers but tonight the only thing I can stand against my battered skin is a sheet. I reach for my phone to turn on music and remember those fuckers nabbed it.

Before the beer grows too warm, I pop it open and drink it in three gulps.

The film inside my head replays those critical seconds when the thugs came out of nowhere. Like a scene from The Matrix, I watch myself in slow motion getting pummeled; I hear Jack's cries, paralyzed by my inability to help either of us.

The next cut is a close-up of my father's face, eyes blazing as if he wants to kill me, and I realize at that moment, the esteemed Dr. Ashton Meadows doesn't give a rat's ass about his son.

Chapter Twenty-Two

A cool hand on my forehead wakes me. "Michael?" The room is dark save for light from the hallway. Jennifer's voice and fingers are soothing. "I want to see if you're okay."

My voice is a gravel road. "I think I'm still alive."

She sits on the edge of the bed. "I'm going to turn on the light and check your eyes. You could have a concussion."

She snaps on the bedside lamp. Instinctively, I close my eyes from its brightness. She gasps when she sees my face but calmly aims a small flashlight in my eyes.

"How's Jack?"

"They put a cast on his leg." She looks into my eyes and asks me to follow the light as she moves it back and forth. "Hopefully he won't chew the plaster off. Otherwise he'll have to wear the cone of shame."

I give her a weak smile. "Do they make them for humans?"

"It's not your fault."

"But it is. I took Jack with me."

"Why did you walk him so late in the evening?"

I try to shrug but my body screams in pain. "He brought me the leash."

Laura Moe

She turns off the flashlight and sighs. "It's really my fault. I didn't have time to walk him today."

"I thought this was a safe neighborhood."

She pats my shoulder. "There's no such thing as a safe neighborhood." She sets the flashlight on the bedside table. "You don't seem to have a concussion, but I still think we should take you to the ER."

"I don't have health insurance."

"Money isn't a problem."

I sure as hell don't want to owe my father for a medical bill. "I'll be okay."

"If you change your mind, I'm happy to take you." She hands me two Aleve capsules and I swallow them with water. "So, what happened?"

"I was texting with Peri, and I guess I wasn't paying attention to the surroundings. These two guys came out of the shadows. One of them had a bat."

"How far away were you?"

"Close to the freeway on Ravenna Blvd."

"You carried Jack all the way home from there?" I nod. "Why didn't you call?"

"They took my phone."

She rests a hand on my arm. "I'm so sorry, Michael. Did they take your wallet, too?"

"I didn't have it with me. Just the phone. And my keys."

"Who's your provider? I'll call and report the theft."

"AT&T, but I'll probably just cancel the contract. I can't afford a new phone."

"We'll get you a new one."

"No! I don't want anything from him."

200

She sighs. "How about if I give you an old one of *mine*?"

"Yeah. Okay."

"Good. If you feel up to it tomorrow, I'll take you to AT&T so they can activate it." She stands and grabs the flashlight. "I'm going to leave your door open. Yell if you need anything."

"Okay."

A few minutes later I hear raised voices coming from their bedroom. I can't hear the words, but Jennifer sounds pissed off.

***

Jack's Cat is snuggled against me when I wake. He gazes at me with his single eye and purrs loudly when I scratch under his chin. "I'm sorry about your buddy," I tell the cat. He head-butts my hand and dashes off when I throw back the sheet.

I dress slowly and take the stairs one careful step at a time, hoping my father is off swashbuckling somewhere. Anywhere but here.

Jennifer stands in the back yard. She's wearing a sun hat, holding a coffee cup in one hand and tossing a spiky rubber ball to Lucy with the other. Thank God Lucy had enough sense to stay home last night.

I open the French doors and stride outside.

Jennifer turns. "It lives!"

"Barely. I feel like the Tin Man after he's been out in the rain."

"There's plenty of coffee left to oil you up with. I'll make you some oatmeal, too. Oats are soft, so they won't hurt to chew."

"That sounds great."

Jennifer tosses the toy far into the yard and follows me back inside the house.

"Where's Jack?" I ask.

"He bit through the cast, so Ash took him back to the vet." Jennifer sets her hat on the counter and digs through the cabinet for oats. She measures half a cup into a bowl and adds water.

I pour myself a mug of coffee and pick up a hot pink phone on the counter. "Your old phone?" She nods. "Cute."

"I'd still prefer to buy you a new one."

Sitting hurts my butt, so I remain standing and prop my elbows on the counter. "I think it's time for me to go back to Ohio."

Jennifer places the bowl in the microwave and hits 90 seconds. "You'll be safe if you don't walk around late at night."

"That's not what I mean." I stretch my arms full length across the breakfast bar. It's both painful and pain relieving. "I think I've worn out my welcome."

Jennifer reaches into the silverware drawer, pulls out a spoon, and looks at me for a long second. Then she switches her gaze to the microwave as the bowl turns around and around. "Do you want honey in it?"

"Honey would be nice. Thanks."

The microwave pings. She grabs the handle of the bowl and sets it in front of me. She hands me a jar of honey and a spoon. "Ash doesn't blame you for what happened."

"Yes, he does." I stir a spoonful of honey into my cereal and take a bite. "You saw how he reacted last night."

She sighs. "Jack's very special to him."

"And obviously I'm not."

Jennifer picks up a rag and wipes imaginary dirt from the microwave door. She dumps the rag in the sink and refills her coffee cup. "Ash was worn out from the party. And seeing Jack injured rattled something in him."

"It was more than that." I stir my oats.

"It just takes a while to know him."

I lift my loaded spoonful. "The thing is, I'm not sure I *want* to get to know him."

"Oh. I see." She sets her mug down and swipes a few stray oats on the counter into her hand. She flicks these in the sink. She picks up the rag again and scrubs at the inside of the sink as if sanding wood. Even with her back to me, I sense Jennifer's upset. She's the last person in the world I want to hurt.

"How was the party last night?" I ask.

She shuts off the water and turns. "It was wonderful. Hundreds of people there. And the view from Columbia Tower at night is fabulous."

"Did you get to meet Bill Gates?"

"We did. He and his wife are lovely people."

"I'm glad you had a good time."

She pushes away from the sink. "I'm headed out for coffee with a couple of teacher friends, but I should be back in an hour or two." She picks up the pink iPhone and hands it to me. "Then we'll get this activated."

After I finish eating, I stumble my way back upstairs and retreat to my room.

I fire up my laptop and pull up the Delta Airlines web site to scan through flights to Columbus. I keep clicking through the menu to figure out how to book a seat and the page freezes. Where's Shelly when I need her? Shit! I'll just go to the airport and let them do it.

In my email is a message from Peri.

What happened? I tried to call you and your phone went straight to voicemail Did you block me?

I respond.

Hi Peri.

I got mugged last night just as I was texting you. They stole my phone, and broke one of Jack's legs. Things here have turned to shit, so I'm going back to Ohio.

I wait for a reply, but email is slower than texting. I message my sister, explain how I got mugged, and add how I plan to come home in the next couple of days. I sign off and glance around.

This room has been my home for two months. Luckily, I haven't accumulated much. I set my blue suitcase on the bed and unzip it. The room wavers and I sit.

I'll leave behind most of the stuff Hunter gave me when we moved out of the dorm. Maybe Jennifer can wear the shirts, and I can ask her to give Shoe the beer fridge when he comes back to Seattle.

Earl and Dot still have a space for me in their home, so I'm not homeless.

Someone taps on my door. "Come in," I say, expecting Jennifer. But my father stands in the doorway. What the hell does *he* want?

We stare at one another for a beat. He clears his throat. "Jack's going to be okay once the bone heals."

"That's good. I'll pay you back for the vet bills."

He waves it off. "We have pet insurance."

I shuffle to my feet. "Listen, I'm flying home soon, so your life can get back to normal."

He glances at the open suitcase on the bed. "You don't have to leave, Michael."

"Yeah, I think I do."

He bites his lip, and says, "Jennifer's downstairs waiting to take you to the phone store."

"Tell her I'll be down in a minute." He turns to leave, and I add, "You know what?"

He stops and regards me. "What?

"I spent my whole life looking for you, yet it seems to have been a giant waste of time, because when you look at me, all you see is trash, like the kind that washes up on Pacific Beach. You're afraid to even acknowledge my existence because I'm not *entitled* enough to be the son of the Dr. Oz of the ocean world."

He replies in a raspy voice. "That's not true at all."

"Yeah, right." I grab my shoes. Pain shoots through me and I sit on the bed. "And you know what else? That girl you treated like shit? That girl *loved* you, but apparently I have too much of *her* in me for you to consider me a human being."

"I loved your mother, too."

I stand and face him. "You had a funny way of showing it."

"We were kids." He pauses, and backs out the door.

***

Jennifer offers to let me drive, but the world still wobbles. Our ride to the phone store begins in silence, and I'm pretty sure Jennifer heard everything I said to her husband back at the house. I don't want her to be mad at me. My issues are just between him and me.

"Nothing is your fault," I say. "If it were just you and the animals, I'd be happy to stay forever. But sometimes shit just doesn't go my way."

She glances at me. "Michael, I'm so sorry." She drives a couple blocks, and adds, "I think Ash isn't used to being around a young adult full-time."

"He teaches at a freaking university. He's surrounded by teenagers."

"But he doesn't bring any of them home." She stops at a light and looks at me. "When do you plan to leave?"

"I don't know. I need to see Peri first."

"What will you do when you get home?"

I rest my head on the window. "Lead the rest of my crappy life in Rooster, Ohio."

She squints at me. "Somehow I don't see that in your future. You're bright and resourceful, and in spite of how things turned out between you and Ash, you have many people who love you."

And she's right. My family loves me. They're all flawed in their own ways, but they've always had my back.

"Will you go to school in Ohio?" Jennifer asks.

"I've been offered two years tuition at the branch campus."

"That's a good start."

"And I'm pretty sure I can get my old job back at the movie theatre," I say. "But I'll need to get another car."

"You've had a tough few months, haven't you?"

"*Pffft.* That's been my whole life story. The Netflix series based on my biography is called *Michael's Daily Disaster.*"

Jennifer parks near AT&T. "I just wish things could have been easier for you here." She shut offs the engine and we walk to the store.

Jennifer explains to the phone guy about my stolen phone and asks if her old phone can replace mine. "Did you back up your information in the cloud?" the guy asks.

"No." I always ignored the backup reminders. Then it hits me; I have no pictures left of The Blue Whale. Or Shelly. I also don't have anybody's phone number.

"I'll give you a link where you might retrieve some of your phone data. But we can't guarantee you'll be able to find all your contacts."

"What about photos?"

"I'm afraid those are gone unless you backed them up on your computer." The phone guy is able to retrieve my last text, which gives me Peri's number.

When we walk out of the store Jennifer types her and my father's numbers in my contacts folder. "Will you stay in touch?" she asks.

"With *you*, yeah."

"Come on. I'll buy you lunch." As Jennifer and I stroll across the parking lot, I text Peri. *I have a phone again.*

She calls back. "Are you okay?"

"Yeah, I'm fine."

"Don't believe him," Jennifer says into my phone. "He's a hot mess,"

"I'm just a little bruised."

"Are you home? I can come by after I get off work."

"No, we're at Northgate."

"I'm working until three," Peri says.

"I'll come to the bookstore after we eat."

Jennifer and I go to Panera and I order two different bowls of soup. Jennifer starts the conversation by telling me her book club is reading the first book of the Elena Ferrante series. "We don't normally do series, but one of the women insisted this book is so good we'll want to read all four."

"What's it about?"

"I'm not sure. According to the back cover it chronicles a friendship between two women."

I snort. "A book every guy wants to read." I shovel in a couple spoonsful of tomato basil soup.

"You men are missing out by your refusal to read women authors." She takes a bite of her turkey croissant sandwich.

"I don't *refuse* to read them. It's just... most girl books don't interest me."

"It's male readers that cause many female writers to use initials rather than their names. J.K. Rowling and S.E Hinton were smart to disguise their gender."

I slurp more soup. "Harry Potter is great."

"Did you know the author was a woman when you read it?" she asks.

"I guess it didn't cross my mind. But Harry Potter isn't girlie."

"What if the protagonist had been Hermione? Would you still have read it?"

"Probably not." I pick up the bowl and drink the rest of my soup.

"What's the last book by a female author you read? Not one you *had* to read for a class. One you read for pleasure."

I take a gulp of chicken and rice soup and run through the booklist in my brain. Anthony Doerr, Jack London, Carlos Ruiz Zafon, Haruki Murakami. Jeez. Maybe Jennifer's right. Maybe I am a sexist reader. Wait. "There was a book my Lit prof recommended. *I Called Him Necktie*, by Milena Michiko Flasar."

"Why did you read it?"

"My lit professor, who is female by the way, thought I'd like it."

"And did you?"

"Yeah. It was great."

"Was the protagonist male or female?"

I mumble. "Male."

Laura Moe

"What is your favorite book with a female protagonist and why?"

I think for a minute. "I always thought Hester Prynne was pretty badass. She had more balls than that wimpy preacher. And I always liked Scout from *To Kill a Mockingbird*. And Katniss in *The Hunger Games*."

Jennifer grins and wrinkles her napkin over her plate. "There's hope for you yet."

Chapter Twenty-Three

Jennifer drops me off at Emerald City Books, where I buy a cup of coffee and sit outdoors. Lying on the table is a copy of *The Stranger.*

I'm reading the Savage Love column about a bisexual who needs dating advice when I hear Peri exclaim, "Oh My God, Michael. You look terrible."

I reach up to touch my bruised face. "You should see the other guy. Not a scratch on him."

She tenderly touches my cheek. "I'm so sorry that happened." She scoots up another chair and sets a lunch bag on the table.

"Jack got the worst of it." I explain how one of the dudes broke the dog's leg.

"Is he okay?"

"Yeah, but it's caused a deeper crevasse between the swashbuckler and me."

She pulls a sandwich from her bag. "How?"

"He blames me."

"Why?" She picks up her roast beef sandwich and takes a bite.

I shrug, and utter the words I've known all along. "My father doesn't like me."

"But you guys had a great day together yesterday."

"You didn't see him last night after I carried his dog home." I glance away. "The look he gave me…the first thing out of his mouth was, 'what the hell did you do to my dog?' He spit those words as if he wanted to kill me."

"I'm sure it was just the shock." She takes another bite of her roast beef.

"He never even bothered to ask if *I* was okay."

She swallows more of her sandwich. "Did he apologize?"

"Nope."

Peri scrutinizes me. "So, what happens now?"

"It's time for me to go back to Ohio. I don't really want to, but I don't see my immediate future here."

Her dark eyes well up. "I hate that this happened to you."

"Thanks. And I really like Seattle. But right now, I need to be near my family. People who know me well but love me anyway. You get that, don't you?"

"I do."

"Seattle fits me better than baggy old Rooster, Ohio. But other than you, I have no reason to stay."

She looks down. "I'm sorry about not telling you about my date. But we never said we were exclusive."

I wave it off. "It doesn't matter now."

She sips from her water bottle. "Will you patch things up with Shelly?"

"Maybe."

Peri wads up her napkin. "When do you leave?"

"As soon as I book my flight."

"So, I guess this is it."

"I guess so."

Her chair scrapes the concrete as she stands. "This was only my break so I have to get back to work. Stay in touch, okay?"

I look up. "I will."

She plants a kiss on my forehead and goes inside.

***

I take the bus home and walk around the lake, slower than usual since I'm still bruised. Jennifer gave me another key, so I'm able to get in the house. Neither Jennifer nor my father are home. I creep up the steps and lie down.

Later in the evening, Jennifer checks on me. "How are you feeling?"

"So-so."

"Do you want me to fix you a plate and bring it up for dinner?"

"That would be great. Thanks."

Jennifer brings me a grilled cheese sandwich, potato salad, and a bottle of water. "I figured soft foods would be easier to chew."

After I eat, I swallow two Aleve capsules and nod off.

***

The shouting from the backyard wakes me. I peek through my blinds to see Jennifer and my father facing one another near the fence. She pokes his chest with her finger. "You. Have. To. Fix. This."

My father turns away from her. She grabs the sleeve of his shirt. "You need to tell him! You owe him that!"

He throws his hands up in the air. I don't hear his reply, but I'm nine-hundred-ninety-nine percent sure this about me.

I take a shower, and as I dress, I hear man-sized footsteps coming up the stairs. As I pull my T shirt over my head there's a knock at my door. I consider ignoring it, but he knows I'm in here. "Come in."

My father's skin lacks its usual robust color, and dark circles surround his eyes. Whatever Jennifer told him to tell me is bad. "Hey. Can we talk?"

I just look at him.

He purses his lips. "Please."

"Fine."

He steps inside. I pick up a pair of dirty socks and shove them inside the plastic bag I use for laundry.

My father sits on my bed and plants his hands on his knees. The creases on his forehead are rivers. He motions for me to sit.

I straddle my desk chair, dangling my arms off the back. Pain shoots up my side. He looks around the room as if the words he needs might be hidden inside the walls. "There are some things I need to tell you." He leans forward and I wait for him to continue.

He presses a hunk of his hair back with his fingers. "First I need to apologize for making you feel unwelcome."

"A little late, but okay." I give him a slight nod.

He fixes his gaze on me. Gives me a thin grin. "This whole thing has thrown me for a loop, too."

I don't respond, forcing him to fill the silence. He grips his thighs and examines me. "I didn't have a great relationship with my own father, so maybe I don't know how to act like one."

"What do you mean?"

"He was..." My father glances at the door, and then back at me. "My father loved money, power, cars, and a string of women, in that order. The rest of us, my mother included, were way down on his list of priorities.

"He wasn't the kind of dad who played catch in the yard or bounced kids on his knee. Granted, he worked long hours. He and his partner had their hands in all kinds of business ventures.

"Materially, we lived well. But I would have given up all the toys in my closet just to have him there. I never felt like I knew him as a person. He was more like a distant uncle."

When I don't respond, he adds, "Ironic. I know, since you probably feel the same way about me. I think you told Jennifer that I'm a book written in a foreign language."

"Something like that."

My father crosses his arms. "To those on the outside, my family had it all. We lived in a mansion by a lake. All three of us kids got brand new cars when we turned sixteen. We carried credit cards, traveled to nice places on holidays." He scrapes his fingers through his hair again. "But it was all so empty. My father didn't abuse us. He just wasn't there.

"The only time he showed much interest was when we did well in sports." He gesticulates. "Then he acted like it was *his* accomplishment. Like *he* was the one who trained day in and day out and got his head and body bashed on the football field or ran miles and miles in sticky heat and vaulted over fifteen-foot poles."

He looks down and shakes his head. "He threw money at the school so they named the auditorium after him, but all my brother, sister, and I wanted was for Dad to say 'good show,' or 'great job.' Yet nothing we did was ever quite enough. He pressured us to do better next time."

"Am I supposed to feel sorry for you?" I ask.

"No. That's not my point." He studies me. "He wasn't brutal, he just...my siblings and I were near the bottom of his list."

"How did he treat your mother?"

He uncrosses his arms and stretches his legs out. "Slightly better."

"Why are you telling me this?" I ask.

"I need you to see that I don't really know how to act like a father because I had a lousy example."

"Looks like you're following *his* example to the letter."

He snaps his head back as if I've punched him. "I guess I deserve that."

"If you're trying to get me to like you, it's not working." I clasp my hands behind my head and incline my back against the desk. Pain shoots up my side again but I maintain the pose because I don't want to appear weak. "So, is this what Jennifer told me I needed to know about you?"

"You heard our argument."

I nod toward the open window. "Hard not to."

He knots his fingers together. "Unfortunately, there's more. And it won't make you like me any better, either."

I give him a half smile. "Can't wait to hear this."

He sucks in a deep breath and continues. "Right after I got my doctorate, I interviewed for a position back at Ohio State. It was late spring, one of those perfect days in May when it feels good to be alive, so I didn't mind the long walk from the parking garage on High Street to

BOZO." He grins, and adds, "That's what we called the Botany Zoology building. BOZO."

I want to ask why the hell he's telling me this, but I let him keep talking.

"I took a short cut through Mirror Lake, which is a large grassy area near the commons. It has a duck pond and benches."

"I know," I say. "I've been there."

"Right." He rakes through his hair again. "Anyway, on a day like this it was packed with students. They were lying in the grass, sunning themselves, and if I weren't dressed for a job interview, I might have grabbed a Frisbee or lain down on the grass myself." He tries to smile at me.

I just stare at him.

He clears his throat. "I had a few minutes to spare, so I sat down on one of the benches. It felt nice to reconnect with one of my favorite spots on campus from my under-grad days.

"I scanned the crowd, watched students enjoy the weather, and my eyes stopped on a young couple across the lake having a picnic with their kids." He rubs his palms together and looks down. "The woman was beautiful- thin and blonde-she looked almost like a model. But aside from her physical beauty she radiated something so powerful I couldn't stop looking at her. Something about her felt familiar, and I was a little jealous of the good-looking black man with her bouncing a baby in his lap."

Something inside me clicks.

"I kept watching them," he says. "Because it was impossible not to. The woman was feeding the man because his hands were full with holding the baby." My father wipes his mouth. "At one point the woman burst out laughing, and started chasing the two boys, and I looked more closely...that's when it hit me who she was."

Snapshots pop into my brain. The world was sun warmed, and the smell of summer hovered in the grass. Jeff and I ran barefoot across the lawn, shrieking in laughter. Bob tried to teach Annie to say *Daddy*, but it came out as *doo doo*. Mom fed us egg salad sandwiches and carrot sticks. Then Mom became the tickle monster.As she grabbed for our feet, Jeff and I laughed so hard I got hiccups. Later, Bob took us out for ice cream cones. Mine was fresh strawberry on a cake cone. Jeff dropped his chocolate cone on the sidewalk and I shared mine with him.

I bolt to my bathroom and vomit in the sink.

My father stands behind me. I hiss at his reflection in the mirror. "You knew about me."

He raises his hands as if in defeat.

I swing around to face him. "You fucking *knew* about me!"

His voice judders. "I almost walked over to take a closer look to be sure."

I dry my mouth on a hand towel. "What stopped you? Too low class?"

"No. Not at all. I..." He gathers his words. "I wasn't totally certain." "And your family looked so complete. So happy. I'd never seen your mother so jubilant. I didn't want to break the spell."

"So, you just *left*?"

"I had to. I was on my way to a job interview and I didn't want to be late."

I throw him a look of disgust and push past him.

"I was an unemployed PhD graduate. What would it have served for me to barge in from the past and lay claim on you?"

"Are you fucking *kidding* me?" I snatch my backpack off the floor and slide my computer and power cord inside. "It would have changed my life! But no. You chose to abandon my mother and me all over again."

"I didn't abandon her. I *didn't* know about you until that moment. Even then, I wasn't one hundred percent sure."

"So, you just walked away."

He opens his mouth to speak but all that comes out is a strangled sound. He reaches out to me but I flick his hand away.

"You never cared about her at all, did you?" I say.

"I'll admit I never fully acknowledged your mother when we were in school. And that was shitty of me. But I did love Susan, and when I saw her at the lake that day, with this man who openly adored her and her children, two of which were clearly not his own, I just couldn't ...."

As he talks, I pull a few things off my desk and cram them inside the bag. I leave his autographed book sitting on the desktop.

He continues. "I thought by walking away I was doing you and your mother a favor. Why screw up a good thing?"

I huff. "Except a few months later it all turned to shit." I stash my new pink phone in my back pocket and pick up my sunglasses. I scan the room and stuff a T-shirt, pair of socks and underwear in the outside pocket. I zip all the pockets on my knapsack.

"Was it worth it?" I ask. "Did you get the job?"

"No. I kind of fucked up the interview. All I could think about was that family on the grass."

I stand squarely in front of him. "And all this time you never once looked for me."

"After the interview, I went back to the lake, but you and your family were gone. I didn't know your mother's married name, so I didn't know how to track you down." He looks down. "I guess I missed my chance."

"You *guess*?" I sling the bag over my shoulder and gesture to the door. "Did Jennifer know about this?"

"Not until last night."

I turn to leave and he grips my arm. "I know things between us have not been easy, but it's not about you. It's about *me*, and my guilt."

I wrench my arm from his grasp. "It's always been all about you, hasn't it?" I start down the steps. "I'll let Jennifer know where to send the rest of my shit."

He follows me. "Michael, I want you to stay. I'd like us to start over."

"Too little too late, man. I'm done." I fling the front door open, and turn to look back at him. "All my life I wanted a father, but you? You're not that guy."

Chapter Twenty-Four

I dash toward the lake.

My mother lied to me about his identity all my life. It makes sense now because she knew the truth about him. She once told me, "knowing him will not make your life better." At the time, I thought she was being contrary. Now I see it was her way of shielding me. Ashton Meadows never cared about her, and he doesn't care about his son.

A mile into the run I'm drenched in sweat. I slow my pace and think about my brother's father, Paul. He may be a working-class dude with only a high school education, but he's a far better man than the internationally acclaimed Doctor Ashton Meadows.

Annie's father Bob was a good man, too. He gave my mother joy and he showed me how a real man behaves. He was a good father.

Even crusty old Earl is a good father. He's cranky and demanding, but he's never unkind. He took my sister and me in when we were homeless, and he's never asked for anything in return.

Every man I've known is a better man than my own father.

The pack grows heavier with each step so I shuck it off and lean forward. I take several deep breaths and shuffle over to Peet's, where I order a large iced tea and sit at an outside table to cool my body and brain.

Rooster, Ohio is far from paradise, but at least there I know what's coming next. I'm done with high wire acts and disasters.

What's stopping me from leaving right now? I've got a credit card, my computer, and most of the important stuff. From here I can catch a bus downtown and take the light rail out to the airport.

I stand, shoulder my pack, and head toward the bus stop. My phone buzzes.

It's an Ohio number, but since I lost my contacts, it could be anybody. I tap Accept. "Hello?"

"Hi," a girl's voice says.

"Annie?"

"Neruda, it's me!"

I stop walking. Only one person in the world calls me Neruda. Hearing her say it now is salve on an open wound. I let out a long breath. "Shelly."

"Did you delete my number?"

"No. My phone got stolen and I lost all my contacts."

"What are you doing?"

"At the moment I'm heading to the airport to book a flight back to Ohio."

"Don't," she says.

"Why not?"

"I'm in Seattle."

I swallow the ice cube that was melting in my mouth. "What are you doing in Seattle?"

"I wanted to talk to you."

"You couldn't text or email?"

"It's kind of complicated on the phone," she says.

"If you're pregnant, what makes you think *I'm* the father?"

"Really, Neruda? *That* again?"

"What the hell is it then?"

"Just come meet me," she says. "I wouldn't ask if it weren't important."

"Are you at Theo's?"

"No. I'm staying in a hotel downtown."

I slurp the remaining iced tea. "Okay. Tell me where you are."

"Meet me at a place called The Crumpet Shop. It's next to Left Bank Books."

As I wait for the downtown bus, I question if meeting Shelly is a good idea. Didn't she wreck me once? But I'm already in hell. How much more damage can she do?

I wander through the crowds at Pike Place Market and find The Crumpet Shop. Shelly is seated at a small table near the entrance of the narrow tea shop, her head bent toward a book. Some of the despair I've been lugging around dissipates at the sight of her.

Her hair has grown out from the purple pixie to a shoulder-length, golden blonde with dark roots. She now resembles the girl in the family portrait hanging in her parents' family room.

I slide into the chair across from hers and dump my bag on the floor.

She raises her head and gasps. "Oh my God, Neruda! What happened to you?"

"What do you mean?" Then I remember my bashed-in face. "Oh, yeah, I got mugged a couple nights ago."

She gently places her fingers over my bad eye. "Are you okay?"

"I'll live." I shrug. "Your hair looks good. How did it grow so fast?"

She reaches up and fluffs it with her fingers. "It's a wig."

I rest my elbows on the table and gaze squarely at her. "So, you don't answer any of my texts, but you fly all the way to Seattle just to have a cup of coffee with me?"

She smirks. "Actually, I'm drinking tea."

I roll my eyes and glance at the menu board. There are about a hundred and fifty different types of tea listed. "Do they have coffee?"

"I think they might smuggle you a cup."

"You want something to eat?" I ask. The rhythm of sitting here with Shelly feels like we picked up where we left off- before the shit-storm over Theo.

She gazes at the menu on the wall. "I've heard the lemon curd and ricotta crumpets are to die for."

She reaches inside her purse, but I stop her. "My treat for once."

"Okay. I'll take a lemon curd crumpet."

She refills her tea cup as I order. After I sit down, I ask, "So what do you need to talk to me about that you couldn't send in an email or text?"

Shelly takes a small bite of her crumpet and sets her fork down. "There are things I need to say to you, and I thought they would be better said in person."

Her parents bathe in money, so I guess flying across the country just to chat and drink tea is no big deal.

She reaches across the table and touches my hand "First, I'm sorry about ...well, you know. All of it." Her words are shattered and thin. "Can you ever forgive me?"

Her question splinters me. I was sorry about us, too, but no matter what she has to tell me I'm not afraid. She can't hurt me now.

She sips her tea. "I do love you, Michael. Maybe not the way you want me to."

"Is Theo the one you love?"

It takes her some time to answer. "I don't know, Michael. I need to learn to love me before I can truly love anyone else." She taps the side of her cup. "After you fled from me in the airport, I had a major meltdown. My Mom had to fly back from Ohio to get me."

I lean forward and clasp my hands, wondering what I'm supposed to say.

She plays with her fake hair. "But I'm so freaking glad to see you now."

I want to tell her how much I've thought about her the past few weeks, but she crushed me by sleeping with Theo, so I take a bite of the crumpet. "Ummm. This *is* good."

Shelly and I savor our food in comfortable silence. We used to spend hours together, not talking, and that was okay.

"What have you been up to?" she asks.

I wipe my mouth with a napkin and take a slurp of coffee. Even though Shelly would get a kick out of my modeling nude, I don't want to talk about Peri yet. "I ran into Dale at a bookstore and he helped me get a temporary job as a custodian at U dub."

She tilts her head and smiles. "You're morphing into a mini Earl."

I chuckle. "Earl gave me a glowing job reference, and they hired me in spite of my criminal past."

"Are you still working?"

"No. The job ended a few days ago."

"How's Dale doing?"

"Still working menial jobs for research. He seems to like this one, though. He says being a custodian is less dangerous than being a night security guard."

"Does he still make terrible puns?"

"Every day. That's part of his charm." I swallow the last of my crumpet and take a large gulp of coffee. "How come you're not staying with Theo?"

"I haven't talked to him since...well, you know."

I want to say how *could* I know? Yet she flew all the way out from Ohio just to talk to me. "Do you plan to see him while you're here?"

"I don't know. Maybe." She bites into the last of her crumpet and dusts the crumbs from her hands. "I almost forgot. I have a gift for you." She rifles through her giant purse and pulls out a brown envelope and hands it over. "I can't look at these ads and not think of you."

Inside the envelope are several pages of men's cologne ads ripped from magazines. I laugh. "Which one should I wear?" At the moment I reek of sweat.

She studies the pages, and points to Prada Classic. The inside of the flap reveals it sells for 105 bucks a bottle. I rub the page against my neck and chest. "Does my body odor smell expensive now?"

She sniffs. "Ummmm, not bad."

"Thanks." I cram the rest of the samples in my bag. "Is this why you flew across the country? To give me samples of expensive men's cologne?"

She swirls the spoon around in her tea cup. "I'm seeing a therapist again, and she says I need to make amends. Besides apologizing to you, Michael, I need you to understand why I'm kind of a mess."

"I already know."

"You only know part of it."

"Okay. Tell me what I don't know"

She sets the spoon on the table, cups her fingers around her tea, and sips. "My first memory is of sitting on carpet in the living room of our Cleveland house. I think I was two. I recall being cold and wet. It was winter and my clothes and hair were soaked."

She sets the cup on the table. "There's an image in my head of two women standing face to face. My mom and my mother. My mom picked me up and placed me in a chair. She dried my hair with a pink sweater." Shelly tilts her head and forms a half smile. "I remember the sweater because it was the most delicious pink, like cotton candy, so pink I wanted to eat it.

"Anyway, the woman—my mom--wrapped me up like a taco in a terry cloth robe that must have smelled of roses because every time I smell roses I think of that robe. She held me on her lap. 'Stay the night,' Mom said, to the woman at the door.

"I have a fuzzy image of a thin woman with long, wet hair-- her face kind of knotted in pain. She said something to my mom, but it's in memory, so whatever she said sounded like someone talking underwater.

"In the next image, I see snow falling like tiny angels in the front porch light. The wet woman shakes her head and walks out through the open door. I try to scramble after her but Mom holds me back. I think I was crying." Shelly pauses. "I'm sure I was crying.

"Then the door closed, and that's the last time I ever saw my mother."

Shelly wrings her fingers together; her voice is almost a whisper. "This memory haunts me because, if I had just been able to reach her, I could have stopped her from leaving and she might still be alive."

I hold Shelly's hands in mine. "You can't blame yourself for her choices."

Shelly takes one of her hands back and wipes her face with her palm. "In my head I know that. But the memory...it's kind of driven my life the past couple of years. I mean, for years I placed the image on hold and lived my life, and Mom and Dad and Josh were my family. But when I found out they really weren't, that night came flooding back, and I can't stop my brain from remembering. And I can't stop looking for that woman who walked away from me."

"But you know she died."

"Technically, I know that. But my therapist helped me see I'm still trying to find pieces of her in my relationships."

"In what way?"

"For one, I'm drawn to guys who have little impulse control. I met Theo on the internet and he and I agreed to drive across the country together before we even met. And then I hooked up with you during community service knowing you had committed a crime."

"You think I'm dangerous?"

She crosses her arms and gazes at me. "You tried to blow up your best friend's car."

"I'd say that makes me more stupid than dangerous."

"You also lived in your car for almost a year. That's a special kind of crazy."

I stare into my coffee cup. "It was a practical solution to my dilemma."

"Maybe," she says. "But it also shows you take risks. Coming to Seattle was a big gamble."

"Yeah." I huff. "It ended up with me falling into quick-sand."

As a couple shoves past us on their way out of the narrow tea shop, the woman's handbag whacks Shelly on the back of the head. The woman seems oblivious.

I pop up, and yell as they exit, "Nice apology, jerk." I give the woman the stink eye.

Shelly reaches for my arm. "Michael, it's okay. Sit down."

I unclench my fists and slump into my chair. "They were assholes."

"Yeah, but it's not worth you getting punched over."

I swipe my hair away from my face. "I guess I see what you mean about me being impulsive. But you hopped on a plane just to see me, so you're a little dangerous, too."

She gives me a sad smile. "Before I found out I was adopted, I was pretty much a color-inside-the-lines kind of girl. But something inside me exploded when I learned the truth about myself."

It's surreal sitting with Shelly now—the one who shackled me to her—and then snapped the chains that bound us. I should hate her. I did hate her. But I don't hate her anymore. I reach over and caress her face. "As much as you've crapped on me, I'd still take a beating for you."

She rests her cheek against the back of my hand. "Of all the people I've hurt, you're the one I most regret."

I study her, hunched forward and vulnerable. This version of Shelly only surfaces now and then. "Aren't we a sorry looking pair?"

"I think you look worse."

"Ha. No doubt," I say.

She takes one of my hands. "It's probably too late for us to be a couple again, isn't it?"

I gnaw on my other knuckle as I consider this. I don't want to lie. My life overflows with liars, beginning with my own mother. It may be easier to count those who have told me the truth than those who have told me outright lies, half lies, and lies of omission.

Shelly once told me if it weren't for lies neither of us would survive. I had to lie to protect my sister and mother, and Shelly had to lie to protect herself. "A lot has happened since that day at the airport."

"Are you seeing someone else?"

"I was."

Shelly drops my hand and tinkers with her spoon. She hides her face behind her shaggy wig.

"You made it clear you wanted to move on," I say. "You practically pushed me away."

Her eyes well up. "I did."

"Shelly, I never would have started seeing Peri if I thought you and I…"

"You're right." She straightens her posture. "My therapist told me I shouldn't be in a relationship right now anyway. So, it's okay. We'll just be friends." She says this too brightly. Her eyes are flickering candles.

"You said that's what you wanted."

"I'm not sure what I want anymore." She stands. "Let's get out of here." Shelly shoulders her bag and rushes through the door. I guzzle the last of my coffee and follow her outside, almost losing her in the jumble of tourists ambling through Pike Place Market. Even today, when it's raining and brisk, the market is engulfed in tourists.

When I catch up to her, I ask, "where are we going?"

"I needed some air."

"Shelly." I try to put my arm around her and she shrugs me off. She heads up the block and we stop in front of the Four Seasons Hotel.

Shelly stops at a platform overlooking Puget Sound. She glances at my overloaded backpack. "Are you really planning to leave today?"

"Yep. All I need to do is head to the airport and change my ticket."

She grips the rail. "Things with your father aren't working out?"

"Hardly."

She shivers and touches her damp wig. "Let's get out of the rain."

We enter the lobby of the Four Seasons and the noise of Seattle gets buried in thick carpet and plush furnishings. It's like walking into a cathedral. This is not the kind of place a white trash guy from Rooster, Ohio stays. At least I smell like I belong here by wearing $105 a bottle cologne.

Shelly strides to the elevator and pushes the up arrow.

"Do your parents know you're here?" I ask. I'm no expert on hotels, but a night in this place won't be cheap.

"They suggested I make the trip."

The doors whisk open and we step aboard. The elevator takes almost no time to climb before the doors swish back open. On the sixteenth floor, Shelly and I exit and walk toward her room.

She dips into the bathroom and I dump my bag on the floor near the desk. I look around and give a low whistle. "This bed should have its own zip code."

"Have you ever been inside a hotel before?"

"We stayed in a Motel 6 when we visited some of Bob's relatives in Pittsburgh." I scan the room. "It was nothing like this, though. It even smells rich in here."

Shelly comes back from the bathroom holding two towels and hands one to me. "So why are you in quicksand?"

I buff my hair with the towel. "The day he met me, he asked me to stay. But as soon as I moved in, it's like he found reasons not to be in the same room with me."

She slips off her flip flops and plops onto the ginormous bed. She sets two pillows behind her and rests against the padded headboard. "That's so sad, Neruda." She wipes her face and arms and tosses her towel to the floor.

"It wasn't all bad," I give my hair one last rub and drape the towel over the back of the desk chair. "I get along great with his wife and their pets. And he and I had a good couple of weeks."

"But overall you didn't hit it off?"

I kick off my shoes and join her on the bed. I grip my ribs where the mugger kicked me. "Don't get any ideas. I just needed to not be standing."

She lightly shoves me. "Continue your story, Perv."

I shove her back and grin. "When I read his latest book and got him talking about his work, he kind of opened up. But just when things were going great, the shit hit the fan."

"What happened?"

"First of all, the whole time I lived with them, my father never *once* introduced me to anyone."

"That's odd."

"Jennifer did. She even took me to her book club one night. In fact, I ran into Theo there."

"I know. You wrote to me about that," Shelly says.

"I did?"

"In your email."

"Oh. I guess I sent that one."

"There were others?

"Yeah. I deleted them."

"Why?"

I shrug. "I don't know."

"Go on."

I cross my arms. "Anyway, my father always kind of kept me at arm's length until I read his book. And once we got to talking about oceanography, he was nicer to me. He even took me out to see the ocean a couple of days ago."

"What did you do there?"

"Walked around on this deserted beach and drove back."

"The same day?"

"Yeah."

"Why?"

I shrug. "It may have been Jennifer's idea for him to spend some time with me, but we had a good time."

"Did you at least talk to each other?" she asks.

"Yeah. He told me about his childhood in Ohio. And he talked a little about my mom."

"Do you feel like you know him any better?"

"Yes and no. He has walls, but at least he didn't treat me like a dead houseplant anymore. That is, until a couple of nights ago."

"What happened?"

"My father and Jennifer have two dogs. Lucy and Jack, and he's freakishly attached to Jack. He's had him since he was a puppy."

Laura Moe

She narrows her gaze. "Did you do something to his dog?"

"Not me! But the muggers did." I give her the Spark Notes version of what transpired that night. "There I am, lying on their front porch bleeding to death, and he acts like *I'm* the one who beat Jack with a baseball bat."

"You did say he's known the dog longer."

I squint at her. "Do you want to hear my story or not?"

She snuggles against me. The weight of her body near mine is something I've missed. And she smells soft, like flowers and honey. "Wait a minute." I jerk my head back. "You don't smell like cigarettes."

"I quit smoking again".

"I thought you were addicted to nicotine."

"My mom found some herbs that have been helping me." She squeezes my arm. "Continue your story."

"Oh, it gets better. This morning he admitted he *had* known about me."

She gasps, and looks at me. "He *did*?"

"He *claims* he didn't know my mother was pregnant in high school, but when I was around six or seven, he saw me with her in Columbus."

"Did she prevent you from meeting him?"

"No. Mom didn't even know he saw her."

"Where was this?"

I massage my thighs as I talk. "Bob and Mom often took us kids for picnics at Mirror Lake on OSU campus. One day my father was there at the same time. He spotted me across the lake."

"Did he talk to you or your mother?"

"Nope. He just walked away."

"Why?"

"He didn't want to be late for a job interview."

Shelly lays her head on my shoulder. "Oh, Neruda."

"He fucking lied to me, Shelly." I clamp my hands down hard on my legs to keep myself from getting emotional. My voice wavers. "The bastard knew about me all along."

"I'm so sorry, Michael." Her fingers wind over my gnarly knuckles. "When did he tell you this?"

"About an hour ago." I reach into the side pocket of my shorts and pull out a couple of antacids. "It shouldn't surprise me."

"Why?"

"Look how he treated my mother." I cross my arms over my chest. "A zebra doesn't change its stripes."

"What are you going to do?"

I shrug. "Go back to Ohio and pretend this whole thing never happened."

"You can't do that."

"Why not?"

"Because you'd never forgive yourself by leaving this unresolved."

"There's nothing *to* resolve," I say. "I belong back in Rooster."

"But you aren't the same Michael Flynn Neruda you were three month ago."

"Yeah. I'm a way more defective version."

She looks up at me with her sparkly, blue eyes. "You and I are like mismatched parts of a broken toy, aren't we?"

Laura Moe

"We are the wretched life forms of which great stories and plays are written." I bump my shoulder against hers. "Yet our chapters keep getting caught in the shredder and pasted in the book upside and backwards."

She rewards me with a thin smile and wraps her hands around my arm. My skin has missed her touch. "I'm glad I know you, Michael Flynn Neruda."

The Michael Flynn Neruda of three months ago would kiss her right now, but too much *has* happened. Shelly's the one person in the world who knows my entire history. She accepted that my mother is a hoarder and never judged me. She was inside the house with me when we found my mother's diary that spelled out how and where I was conceived. She was there for me when I wept after reading how my father dismissed my mother as his hidden treasure. Shelly's been there for me in some of my worst moments, even though she also created a few. "I'm glad I know you, too."

She buries her face in my shoulder. "So where do we go from here?"

"I don't know about you, but I'm headed to the airport."

Shelly sits up and squares her gaze at me. "No. We need to fix this."

"There's nothing to fix."

"He's your father."

"No, he impregnated my mother. He's nothing else."

"Michael, you came all the way out here to establish a relationship with him."

"I came here to take a writing workshop that *you* found online with the *possibility* of meeting my father. I accomplished both. End of story." I slide off the bed and go pee. When I come out of the bathroom, Shelly's standing at the at the window. I reach behind her and rest my chin on her head. "This view is spectacular. We're definitely not in Rooster."

She reaches behind her and grabs my hands and wraps them around her waist. "You can't go back home yet."

"Yes, I can."

She drops my hands and faces me. "Michael, if you leave now, your story won't have an ending."

"The last chapters of the Michael Gillam Flynn Neruda saga washed away in a terrible flood. I have to completely rewrite them."

"But I have a copy of that story, and according to *my* book, Michael Neruda grows a pair and deals with his father."

I back away and toss my hands in the air. "That asshole lied to me. I don't want anything to do with him."

"What did you expect from him?"

"I didn't expect for him to treat me like something he pulled out of the recycle bin."

"But how did you think he *would* treat you?"

I grab my backpack off the floor and chuck it over my shoulder. "It's over. Okay? I'm headed to Sea-Tac."

She plops onto the bed. "Avoiding the truth is always a good idea."

"What the hell does that mean?"

She crosses her arms. "One thing I've learned in therapy is I do crappy things because I'm running from the truth."

"What truth is that?"

"In my case, I'm afraid I'll end up like my birth mother. And the irony is that all the shit I was doing guaranteed I *would* end up like her."

My bag slides off my shoulder onto the floor. "I'm not trying to avoid being like my mother."

"But you are your mother's son. And like her, part of you believes you don't deserve your father's full consideration."

I snatch my backpack. "A couple weeks of therapy doesn't make you an expert on psychology." I fling the door open and stalk down the hallway. Halfway to the elevator I stop, turn around, and bang on her door.

When she opens it, I charge in. "Why the hell did you come here? To lord your psychological superiority over me? "

"No, Michael. I feel bad about all the shit I put you through. And I want you to understand why I'm a hot mess."

I shove past her and dump my pack on top of the dresser. "Not everything between us went wrong."

"True, but the last part was a train wreck." Her voice gets all edgy. "You're the one person I feel I can be totally honest with, yet I hurt you the most."

I flop onto an overstuffed chair that resembles a small bed and lie back.

She scrunches herself next to me. "In your email you said you came here to find a part of your missing family, but what you really came to find is what's missing inside of you."

"What am I missing?"

"You believe you're not good enough."

"Good enough for what?"

"To be treated well."

I gaze out the window. "Peri said almost the same thing, that I believe I deserve to be mistreated."

The giant Ferris wheel turns below us. "You *are* good enough, Michael. Out of the thousands of applications, they chose you for the writing workshop, and they gave you a full scholarship."

"That just proves I can write." I say. "It doesn't mean I'm a worthy human."

"Earl wouldn't have let you work off your community service at the school if he hadn't seen something decent in you. And he *never* would have let you inside his house, either."

"So, I'm not a total waste of skin?"

Shelly squeezes me and strokes my hair. "Subconsciously, you believe you're not good enough to be loved by your father. But Neruda, you got here without him."

I ponder that for a sec. "I did, didn't I?"

"You totally did."

"Fuck him!" I shout.

"Exactly!" Shelly says. "Fuck him!"

I pump my fist. "Being the son of Dr. Ashton Meadows is no big deal!"

"*He's* privileged to be the father of Michael Gillam Flynn Neruda!"

Shelly and I shout back and forth until we laugh so hard, we're out of breath. "I'm going to get you thrown out of this fancy ass hotel."

"*Fuck* them!"

My phone buzzes. I stare at the screen. "It's Jennifer."

"Answer it."

"What if it's *him* and he borrowed her phone?"

She pushes my shoulder. "Answer the damn phone, Neruda."

I make a strangled sound and accept the call. "Hello?"

"Michael, are you okay?" Jennifer asks.

"Yeah. I think so."

"Where are you?"

"In a room at the Four Seasons Hotel."

There's a pause, then she says. "I was hoping you and I could sit down and talk."

Chapter Twenty-Five

It's pouring rain when Jennifer stops in front of the hotel, so I'm grateful for the covered pick up zone. I glide
onto the passenger seat. She glances at the hotel. "Is this where you're staying?"

"Shelly's in town. Her parents bleed money."

"They must. It's about five hundred bucks a night." She
pulls away from the hotel into traffic. "I figured you'd be
hungry since you left before eating breakfast."

"I'm always hungry."

She parks in front of a place in Capital Hill called *Peel
the Apple*. "It's a New York style deli," Jennifer says.
"Make sure you order an egg sandwich on a Kaiser roll.
It's their specialty." We dodge raindrops as we dash inside.

She and I both order egg and Swiss, and I add a bowl
of soup. We take a table near the back and sit across from
one another. A waitress sets our coffees down. Jennifer
sprinkles cocoa powder in hers. "I'm sorry about this
morning."

"You have nothing to be apologize for. He told me you
didn't know until last night."

She raises her eyebrows. "It came as an unpleasant
surprise."

I slug down some coffee. "Yeah, well, I finally realized
I should have left a long time ago."

Jennifer reaches for my hand. "Or you could stay and we can work on undoing the damage."

"I don't think this can be undone."

She stirs her drink. "Ash is still trying to process everything. Given his own upbringing, being a family man is not easy for him."

"You're always defending him, even when he doesn't deserve it."

She levels a stern gaze at me. "He's my husband and I love him. And I know him far better than you do."

We stare at one another. Jennifer's my last ally, and I've pissed her off. But her husband isn't worthy of her. Those protestors were right. Ash Meadows *is* a liar.

The waitress brings our food. Eating gives us a good excuse not to talk.

She takes a bite of her sandwich and dabs her mouth. "I understand your need to create distance from us right now. You've been away from your family and friends all summer. But I hope you aren't closing the door on coming back to establish a relationship."

"Is that what *he* wants?"

"It's what *I* want. For both of you."

I stir the spoon around in my vegetable soup. In the background U2 plays *Invisible*. "When my ex-best friend Rick and I had our big blow up, Shelly wouldn't let me rest until he and I made up."

"Why do you think that is?"

"Because she knew it gnawed at me." I swallow a heaping tablespoon of soup. "She also said I should fix things here."

"You and Ash need to fix things together."

"Will you be our referee?"

She eyes me. "You're both intelligent men. You should be able to work things out without my intervention."

I grumble.

She shakes her head. "Two peas in a dysfunctional pod." She loads her fork with salad. "When do you fly back?"

"I was going to leave today, but with Shelly here, I might hang around another day."

"I hope you and Ash will talk before you fly back to Ohio."

"I'll think about it."

"Good. Now let's enjoy the rest of our lunch."

The sun is out when Jennifer and I walk to the car. She hands me her keys. "Do you want one last taste of Seattle traffic?"

I grin, and get in the driver's side. We buckle up and I make a U turn to head back downtown. "I'll miss making U turns. They're illegal in Ohio."

At the hotel Jennifer and I share a fierce hug. "You've got my number. I'm driving Ash to the airport tomorrow afternoon for an evening flight out. Maybe you and he can talk in the morning."

"I'll let you know."

I text Shelly to let her know I'm in front of the hotel. She replies *@Fonte Coffee on 1st. Join me.*

I pull out my phone and follow the directions to the coffee shop.

Laura Moe

Shelly looks up when I sit. "How did it go with your stepmother?"

I cross my arms across my chest. "She wants me to talk to him face to face."

"Good."

I rest my elbows on the table and clasp my hands. "I'm still leaving, whether I agree to see him or not."

Shelly and I spend the afternoon strolling around Pike Place Market. On our way back to the hotel, we buy carry-out from DeLaurenti's and take it up to her fancy room. I open a couple of Diet Cokes from the mini bar.

We sit at the small dining table near the window. A ferry slowly traverses Puget Sound, The Great Wheel rotates, and the usual traffic whizzes below us. "If I lived in this room I'd never go back to Ohio," I say.

She takes a giant bite of her meatball sandwich and wipes her chin. "I wish they'd had a room with a balcony. We'd have an even better view. But this is all I could get at the last minute."

"Do you hear me complaining?"

We eat the rest of our meal in silence. I gather our trash and pull two miniature bottles of wine out of the cooler and pour them into glasses.

Shelly sips from her glass. "How come you haven't changed your flight yet?"

I take a gulp of wine. "I'm not really sure how to do it. I got on the Delta page, but I think I booked the entire airplane and it knocked me off the site."

She shakes her head. "Oh, Neruda. You really are from Rooster, Ohio." She gets up and opens my laptop.

"The first available seats are on a red eye to Atlanta leaving around nine tomorrow night. Then we get into Columbus around eleven the next morning."

"We?"

"I'm coming with you."

I grin. "Book it."

Her fingers click over the keyboard as she enters our information. "We won't be able to sit together. So, you'll have to freak out during take-off on your own."

I give her the finger. She reciprocates.

She shows me our seats on the seating chart. Hers is a middle seat near the wings. I'm clear in the back by the bathrooms. "We can switch if you'd rather be closer to the front of the plane."

I shrug. "It doesn't matter. We'll die no matter where we sit."

She rolls her eyes. "So maudlin, Neruda."

"At least if I need to hurl, I'm closer to the toilet." I stretch my arms in the air and yawn. "Will you see Theo before we leave?"

"I don't know."

"Do you *want* to see him?"

She chews on a couple of fingernails. "Maybe?"

I pick up her phone. "I see you replaced the one I smashed."

"I kind of had to."

I whip out my pink phone. "So did I."

Shelly practically roars, and that laugh is the music I've been craving since we broke up. I place her phone in her hand. "Go ahead and call him. You have plenty of time to see him before we leave."

"You're okay with that?"

"Yeah."

She punches up his number. "Hey, Theo. It's me." She walks out into hall.

I grab the remote and click on the TV. I flip through the channels and land on a rerun of *The Big Bang Theory,* Shelly's favorite show. It's the episode where the guys get stoned on marijuana cookies and Sheldon has to drive Penny to the emergency room. I know way too much about this series.

Shelly taps on the door and I let her in.

"He's meeting me in the bar downstairs in half an hour," she says. "Do you want to come?"

I no longer feel the urge to stuff Theo into a wood chipper, so I say, "Okay."

She notices the TV and gushes. "O-M-G. My favorite episode!" She dives onto the bed.

"You've seen it a hundred times."

She shushes me and we watch the last fifteen minutes. When the show's over, she pops up. "Let's get ready."

She puts on some lipstick and fluffs up her wig. I change out of my stinky T-shirt, put on jeans and my denim jacket. The Prada I smeared on earlier has worn off so I retrieve the envelope of cologne samples and flip through them. The guy in the Bleu de Chanel ad looks too much like Theo. I choose Tom Ford Noir that sells for $125 bucks a bottle.

Shelly sniffs me. "Mmmmm. Woodsy." She checks her wallet. "Do you have your fake ID?"

"I do. How about you, Wanda?"

"I lost that one in Hawaii." She pulls a new ID from her wallet. "Now I'm Valentine Falls." Her birth name, and the name Theo knows her by.

We take the elevator down to the lobby, which is crowded with a bunch of old people in formal wear. Shelly and I weave through them and make it to the lounge entrance. Theo occupies a stool at a tall table by the window, nursing a beer.

Shelly starts to walk toward him, but I stop her. "Hey, I think it's best if you and Theo meet alone. I've made my peace with him."

"Are you sure?"

"Yeah."

She holds out her room key. "Do you want to go back up to the room?"

I shrug. "I think I'll take a walk and decide what to do about my DNA donor."

"At least come and say hello."

I sigh. "Okay."

Theo stands and envelops Shelly in a giant hug. He beams at her. "You look so different since the last time I saw you."

She flicks her fingers through the blonde wig. "It was time to get rid of the vampire hair."

"It looks good."

He and I nod at one another. Shelly pulls out a stool and sits.

"I'm not staying," I say. "I just wanted to stop by and say hi."

He and I shake hands. "It's good to see you again," he says. There's no pretense that he and I will stay in touch. The first time I met him at the airport I wanted to kick his ass. Should have trusted my instincts.

I glance at Shelly. "I'll meet you back in the room later." It's only 8:15, so there's nearly an hour of daylight left. I saunter toward Pike Place Market. Most of the stores are closed, but Left Bank Books is open and I step in for one last visit. In my rush to leave my father's, I left my books behind, so I'll need something to read on the plane.

The smell of old and new books greets me. It's a primeval aroma that tells me I'm home. Even if I don't find anything, meandering through a bookshop will clear my head.

I'll miss this shop and its quirkiness. I climb to the third floor to work my way down.

As I walk up a flight, near the staircase is a poster with a quote by James Baldwin. "Perhaps home is not a place but an irrevocable condition."

Maybe homelessness is my irrevocable condition. Even if I have physical shelter, I wonder if I'll ever find my true home. Maybe that's what growing up is: finding out what constitutes home.

By the time I make it down to the first floor again, it's nearly dark. I pay for a used paperback called *The Snow Child*. It's by a female author, so Jennifer would be pleased.

I hoof it toward the water to catch the sunset. The sun goes down every day, even in Rooster Ohio, yet here the sunsets are spectacular. Hard to believe both places share the same sky.

Shelly texts. *-Back in the room. Where r u?*

Me-On my way.

I tap on her door. She answers wearing an oversized T-shirt and her natural, short hair, which has faded to lavender.

The bed is still made up. "At least I know you didn't bring Theo up here."

She swats me. "Maybe we did it in the lounge chair."

I scrunch my face. "I was planning to sleep on that."

"You're such an idiot."

I give the recliner a close inspection.

Shelly places her hands on her hips. "You're not sleeping in the damn chair. As you pointed out earlier, this bed is the size of a small town." She pulls the covers back and flops down on the side closest to the door. "There's room enough for both of us."

I flex my arms for her. "How are you going to keep your hands off me?"

She rolls her eyes. "I think I'll manage."

I kick off my shoes and socks and drape my jacket across the back of the desk chair. "Just in case, I'll keep my clothes on."

"Suit yourself."

I slide under the sheets on the opposite side and lie on my back. "What did you and Theo discuss?"

She yawns and switches off the lamp. "The meaning of life."

The drapes are still open and the Seattle skyline sparkles beneath us. "Want me to close the curtains?"

"No. I like the lights." She rolls toward me. "By the way, I'm not going away to college this fall."

"Why not?"

"My therapist said it might be good for me to take a gap year and stay close to home. Or take classes at the branch campus. I think she's afraid I'll go off the rails again if I don't have my weekly sessions with her."

"Are you okay with staying in Rooster another year?"

She shrugs. "My therapist is in Columbus, so I get to see civilization once a week."

I snort-laugh.

"How about you?" she asks. "What will you do once you're back home?"

"For now, I'll take classes at the branch and hopefully work at the movie theatre again."

"What about for later?"

I roll to face her. "That part of my story hasn't been written yet."

"I hope parts of it still include me," she says.

My hand grazes her shoulder. "I hope so, too."

She snuggles against me. "Don't get any ideas. I'm just cold from the air conditioning." She tucks her face against my chest. Her words vibrate when she asks, "are you glad you came here?"

"Hmmm. Meeting my father was an epic fail. And you and I broke up in an Oscar worthy scene at an airport Starbucks. But overall? Good things happened."

"Like what?"

"In spite of the crap with Theo, he taught me a shit load about writing. And I met some incredible people."

"Like your girl Peri?"

"Yeah." I flip to my back and stare at the ceiling, illuminated by the Seattle skyline. "She was great."

"How did you break it off?"

"I told her I was leaving. There was no drama."

"Were you in love with her?"

"She's smart and fun and we had a good time together."

But...?"

I turn and pull Shelly against me. "She's not you?"

Shelly scoffs. "Half the time I'm not me, either."

We share a moment of silence.

"What about meeting Jennifer?" she asks. "You like her, don't you?"

"Yeah. Even though my father's a jerk, his wife is awesome. You two would like each other. She reminds me of a sane version of you."

She punches me gently. "What are you going to do about your dad?"

"He's not my dad!"

"Okay, okay. What will you do about your sperm donor?"

I shrug. "I don't know. Meeting *him* was a waste of time."

She sits up and looks at me. "Are you sure? You stayed with him for almost two months."

"I enjoyed being around Jennifer and the pets. And I like Seattle."

"But you and he didn't share *any* good moments?"

I cross my hands over my stomach and stare at shadows on the ceiling again. "We did. Yet each time he and I connected, it still felt as if I were watching from a distance."

"You can't force something that's not there."

I roll toward her. "Maybe that's my whole problem. I expect people to deliver more than they can."

"Do you hate him?"

"I don't know. Maybe. I want him to suffer. I want him to lie awake at night and stew about how he treated my mother back in high school. And how he contributed to her mental illness. I want that to injure him."

"Don't you think Jennifer would suffer, too?"

I bury my face in the pillow and growl. "She'll probably suffer more."

Shelly strokes my hair. "Be the bigger man, Michael. Don't let this ruin you."

I lie flat on my back. "Gah! Am I going to have to spend my entire life forgiving people?"

"Probably. But when we care about someone, we overlook crappy things about them. Your mom pretty much made you raise your siblings. And because of her you were forced to live in your car. But you've never stopped loving her."

I reach out and caress Shelly's lavender hair. "And even though you ripped out my heart and stomped it into microscopic bits, I never stopped loving you, either."

Her face is an inch from mine. "Does that mean you forgive me?"

"Dammit, I think it does."

She burrows her head against my chest.

"But I also hate you," I say. "Even though you may have done me a favor."

"What favor is that?"

"Theo once told me one can't be a great writer until they've suffered heartbreak."

"Are you going to write about us?"

"Hell yes. I'll make a fortune off of you."

Her head bobs against me as she giggles. "I don't deserve you."

"You deserve far worse."

She looks up at me. "Is that any way to talk to the girl who put you up in a five-star hotel?"

Chapter Twenty-Six

A knock on the door wakes me. Shelly, wrapped in a hotel bath robe and wearing her wig, opens the door and a guy wheels a tray inside the room. Shelly signs the check and bounces onto the bed. "Room service!"

I break into a wide smile. "I never want to leave this hotel."

Shelly and I eat at the table by the window. Below us fog hovers over Puget Sound. By the time we finish our eggs, sausage, toast, and coffee, the sun peeks out.

After breakfast, I shower and dress, and dig through the cologne samples. This time I choose Dolce & Gabanna. When I come out of the bathroom, Shelly reads me a text. "Theo says it was good seeing us last night and wishes us a safe journey home."

Shelly zips up her bag and I sling my backpack over my shoulder. "Good-bye fancy hotel room with the awesome view." We head to the elevator.

She checks out, and we step into sunshine.

"Any last-minute sightseeing trips before we leave Seattle?" I ask.

"How about a ferry ride?"

"Okay." Seattle is freakishly expensive, but walk-on ferry rides are less than nine bucks round trip. We buy tickets for the next sailing to Bainbridge Island and board the boat.

Shelly's hair blows upright as we gain speed away from the pier. "Aren't you afraid your wig will fly off?" I ask.

She grabs the long strands and holds it down. "It's all good."

I lean on the railing and cast my eyes on the water. "Do you think you would have liked your mother if you'd met her?"

Shelly presses against me. "I think so. From what my mom says, she was a sweet person."

"So, you take after your father."

She swats me.

"Do you know anything about him?" I ask.

"No, other than he was a musician who od'd on heroin."

I wrap my arms around her squeeze. "We come from good stock, don't we?"

She gazes up at me. "Aliens from the same planet."

When we reach Bainbridge, we're required to disembark before we can re-board. As we wait, I tell Shelly about my mother's letter. "Can I see the love note?"

I extract it from the side pocket of my pack and hand it to her.

She reads it and gives it back. "Awww. He really did love her."

I refold the note and stash it with the letter. "You think so?"

"He wanted to run away with her."

The gates open and we re-board the ferry. We stand on deck, and as the ship moves the sea air frees up space in my head.

I think about the transitory nature of love and how random it is. There's no foolproof method or plan. On shows like *The Bachelor*, which my sister and Dot watch, not me, contestants try to force love to happen. I think real love is an ineffable energy between two people that sends your endorphins in overdrive, and when they're out of your realm, you suffer. On paper, Shelly and I should never have worked. We're fire and wind. But as I glance at her now, I think of how she and I are like stones on the beach, washed in side by side by a wave.

With the wind slapping my face, I take Shelly's hand. "Okay, I'll talk to my father."

Shelly squeezes my fingers and rests her head on my shoulder. I pull out my phone and text Jennifer. *-If he wants to talk, we can meet at the airport.*

J-*What time is your flight?*

Me-*A red eye. Plane leaves @ 9:05.*

J-*Ash has a 7:10 PM to Miami. He will meet you somewhere inside the terminal before his flight.*

Me-*Are you coming?*

J -*No. You're big boys. Work it out.*

Me- ☹ *OK.*

J -*He'll text you when he gets there.*

I stash my phone in my pants pocket. "The sperm donor and I are meeting at the airport this afternoon."

A few seconds later, my phone buzzes and I pull it out.

J -*Michael, I treasure the time we spent together. I hope you decide to come back for an extended stay.*

Me-*Thanks. You're a great friend. And my favorite stepmother.*

Once back in Seattle, Shelly and I stop for another dose of lemon and cheese crumpets. Then we head to

Westlake Station and catch the light rail to the airport. By the time we make it past security, it's after three.

"We have plenty of time to kill," Shelly says. "Let's get something to eat at the Delta Sky Club."

"What's that?"

"Something my rich parents pay extra for."

Shelly flashes identification and signs me in as her guest. Inside, it resembles a hotel lobby. It also includes a food buffet, so we load our plates and find seats.

"Which are you more nervous about?" she asks. "The flight? Or talking to your sperm donor?"

"Both?"

"Do you know what you're going to say to him?"

I shrug. "Not a clue."

Around 4:30, we stop at a newsstand where Shelly buys a couple of magazines. I see a *New York Times* article speculating Pablo Neruda was murdered, so I purchase a copy.

My phone buzzes at 4:42. "It's him."

HIM-*Going through security now. Where are you?*

"Where should I tell him to meet us?" I quickly add, "Anywhere but that Starbucks. Too much bad mojo."

Shelly pulls up the airport map on her phone and points to a nearby spot.

Me-*In the B gates. At the Taproom*

Shelly and I walk toward the pub. She offers to wait for me at Starbucks or McDonald's, but I tell her, "I'd like you nearby. You may need to keep me from stabbing him."

She rolls her eyes. "He might feel ambushed if we're together."

Laura Moe

"Just stay in proximity."

We find two tables near each other outside the entrance. She sits at her table and I stash my bag at my feet and scope out the surroundings.

Shelly opens a magazine. "This is weird."

"It's like we're undercover spies."

"You'd make a terrible spy," she says. "Someone would offer you food and you'd reveal *all* the secrets."

"Ha ha. Probably true."

Shelly gazes at the crowd. "Is that Subject Zero approaching?"

I look up and spot my father pulling a bullet gray roller bag behind him. He's wearing a leather blazer, a black T-shirt, and jeans. I see what Peri means about him having swagger. He's luminous, gliding through as if he owns this airport, and people, mainly women, give him second glances. For a split second, I worry Shelly will fall under his spell and fly off to wherever he's going.

He sees me, nods, and steps up to the bar. He places an order and points in my direction.

Shelly texts. -*OMG! He's your old clone!!!*

I give her a half smile and set my phone face down. My father walks toward me, parks his bag, and sits down. "I ordered us a couple of beers."

"Thanks."

"Thank you for meeting with me."

"No problem," I say. "I kind of had to be here anyway."

The waitress delivers our drafts and offers a food menu. "I don't care for anything," he says. He glances at me and I shake my head.

260

He and I fill the silence by sipping from our beers. This meeting is his idea, so I'll let him begin.

He clears his throat. "Jen said you had someone with you."

"She's not far."

He glances at Shelly, who pretends to be reading *The Star*. He takes a pull from his brew. "You have every right to be upset. I would be, too."

I tilt my glass and take a drink. "I guess I half understand why you walked away. You didn't know my life would get flushed down the toilet a few months later." I lean toward him. "But here's what I don't understand. You invited me to stay, yet the whole time I was here, you treated me like a trespasser."

He sits back in his chair, his right hand wrapped around the beer glass. He fumbles the cocktail napkin with his left. "As a scientist, the approach is to identify a problem, make sense of it, and explore solutions. It's much harder to make sense of human beings."

"So, I was a science problem?"

"No. I ..." His lips form a tight grin and he swigs his beer. "I wish Jen would have come. She's better at this." He signals to the waitress to bring him a refill. He has lost much of his swagger.

"Did you use your scientific approach with her when you met?"

He taps on his nearly empty glass and gives me a half smile. "It was easy with Jen. Biological attraction kicked in."

"Yeah, you're not my type either," I say.

He chuckles and drains the rest of his beer. The waitress sets down a fresh one. He mutters a thank you and takes a long gulp. He wipes his mouth with the cocktail napkin.

We're surrounded by the clink of silverware on plates and murmured conversations. A man laughs heartily and someone's phone chimes.

"Your appearance came at an inopportune time in my life," my father says.

"Inopportune."

"It means..."

"I know what the word means," I snap.

His face transforms into that confused kid in his high school yearbook, the kid whose own father was incapable of parenting.

Did he do the right thing by walking away?

How different would my story be if my father had strolled across the grass that afternoon at Mirror Lake? Would he and Mom have agreed to share custody of me, where I'd have travelled the globe with him? Would I see my cousins at family reunions and visit my grandmother on Christmas? Would I be named Michael Meadows?

But my story can't be rewritten. Bob still would have died, my mother still would have plunged into an abyss, and my father never would have made that trek across the lake.

He's not that brave.

Last night Shelly said carrying resentment inside weighs too much. Mine weighs ten thousand pounds and anchors me in purgatory.

But the man across the table is not an ogre or a god. Dr. Ashton Meadows longs to save the world from itself, one plastic water bottle at a time, but he's also a guy with limits, and I no longer care whether he suffers or not.

I rise, ten thousand pounds lighter, and extend my hand to him. He looks up, surprised, and then clasps it in his own.

I pick up my phone and shoulder my bag. "Good luck on your lecture tour. And thanks for the beer. Thanks for everything."

Shelly scoots out of her seat and lays a ten-dollar bill next to her water glass. I take her hand and together, we walk out of the airport bar.

I still don't know what my future will look like or where I'll end up, but I know this: Ashton Meadows and I share biology. Someday I will develop his stance, his voice, and the grey streaks in his hair. Maybe I'll even develop swagger.

But I am not my father's son. And that's okay.

#

Do you want to know more about Michael and Shelly's relationship?

Read how it all began in <u>BREAKFAST WITH NERUDA</u>, **2016, Simon & Schuster, ISBN 9781440592195,** and how it derailed in <u>BLUE VALENTINES</u>, **2019, ISBN 9781073346783**

See my website to read *The Dirt Thief* by Michael Gillam Flynn www.lauramoebooks.com

THE AUTHOR and writing partner Pablo would like to thank all the fans of BREAKFAST WITH NERUDA and BLUE VALENTINES who wanted to keep the story going. Special thanks to Sharman Badgett-Young, Jennifer Bardsley, Louise Cypress, Ashley Nicole Conway, Karen McKay Wardle, and Penelope Wright. Also, a shout out to The Barnes & Noble Café at Alderwood.

While some locations and events are real, Emerald City Books, Evergreen High School, Campus Joe, The Skeptics of Science, and Rooster, Ohio are fiction.

65838422R00162

Made in the USA
Columbia, SC
19 July 2019